A Young Songbird's Story

A Young Songbird's Story

A Singers Battle for Her Soul

Jannise R. Childs

ACKNOWLEDGMENTS

As I wrote this book, I have loving memories of my parents Robert Childs and Henriene Patrick Childs. As life has presented me with a few bumps and bruises, rest assured that I've overcome them all, and I still strive every day to make you proud. Please know only because of the love you both demonstrated to me, both Lorin and I are doing fine.

I am thankful for my family and friends, especially my lovely daughter, Lorin Childs, my sister-in-law, Teresa Conley, and my sisters, Larita Kaye Mallory and Phyllis Diane Adams, for always having encouraging words and being my motivation. To my cousins Malinda Christian, Miranda Benjamin, and Shawna Stewart, thank you for the positive reviews of A Songbird Story, a Singer's Intense Battle for her Soul. I cannot begin to tell you how much you warmed my heart.

Please know that I love and appreciate you all.

Jannise R. Childs

A Young Songbird's Story:
A Singers Battle for Her Soul

This book is a re-published work of Author Jannise R. Childs
(A Songbird Story: A Singer's Intense Battle for Her Soul)

Written by: Jannise R. Childs

ISBN: 978-965-578-898-3

Cover Image and Photography Created by: H2 Infinity.com

Cover Design: H2Infinity.com

Cover Image Model: Lorin Childs / Wealthregardless.com

Author's Company: "What A Story Publications LLC"

Author Contact Information: JrChilds@whatastorypublications.net

Publisher Contact: Spines.com

Published by Spines
ISBN: 978-965-578-898-3

PREFACE

In A Young Songbird's Story, a singer's battle for her soul, Jannise R. Childs creates an amazing story. It is one that brings you to what some consider as close as it gets to the real life of a young teenager who is determined to become one of the most influential singers in the music industry. And yes, many have played with the idea of the same old desire and the rise and fall of many. Sex and drugs play an explicit role in almost every entertainer's journey. A Young Songbird's story is more than a mere glance into a tortured soul. In this story, we find that our main character, Lizzah's fate is not sealed like so many of the others. In the moments when she is about to lose the battle, grace finds her, and she is given another chance to get things right. While you travel from page to page, you are provided with more than enough dramatic reading material for a gripping, involving, and emotion-packed book. From the experiences with family and friends to the dark side of self-torture and regret, what emerges from this fascinating author is a valuable lesson through entertaining reading.

This book is a re-publication of Jannise's original book: A Songbird Story: A Singer's Intense Battle for Her Sou.

Contents

A Young Songbird's Story: A Singers Battle for Her Soul

CHARACTER LISTINGS

<u>**Main Characters**</u>

Lizzah Adkins Singer Stage name (Lizzah)

Robin Adkins - Mother of Lizzah Adkins

Henry Adkins - Father of Lizzah Adkins

Timothy Jonnigan (TJ) - Group Leader of the Band and Lizzah's First Love

Corrine Palmer - Lizzah's best friend and confidante

Ada Grace James - Daughter of Stephen James, Lizzah's good friend and business partner

Sebastian Edwards - Goldwings Keyboard Player, Husband of Lizzah

Ralph Leftridge (Preacher Boy) - Goldwings Musician and Pastor of The Open Door Ministry

Stephen James (a/k/a) Pappa J - J-Music Giant and founder of Jamestown Recordings, Father of Ada Grace James

A Young Songbird's Story: A Singers Battle for Her Soul

CHARACTER LISTINGS

<u>Introductory Characters</u>

Milton Yarborough - Introductory Character Main

Melissa Yarorough - Deceased Mother of Milton Yarborough

John Yarborough - Deceased Father of Milton Yarborough

Odessa Dupree - Caretaker and Guardian of Milton Yarborough

<u>Minor Characters</u>

Hiram Blandon - Music Professor LA Conservatory, Paternal Parent of Lizzah Adkins

Towanna Graham - Music Student and Actress– LA Conservatory

Maternal Birth - Parent of Lizzah Adkins

Dr. Ulysses Graham - Father of Towanna Graham

Rose Graham Foote - Sister to Dr. Ulysses Graham and Aunt to Towanna

Patrick Malone - Rising Star and Lead Singer of The Malone Family Band

Stevetta Johnson - Wonderette and Childhood friend of Lizzah Dee

Britt Tovarres - Wonderette and Childhood friend of Lizzah Dee

Liz Malone - Lizzah's High school Friend and Niece of Patrick Malone

Conchita "CoCoa" Malone - Lizzahs High school friend and niece of Patrick Malone

Lonnie Warren - Twin Brother to Ronnie Warren and Goldwings Musician

Ronnie Warren - Twin Brother to Lonnie Warren and Goldwings Musician

A Young Songbird's Story: A Singers Battle for Her Soul

CHARACTER LISTINGS

<u>**Minor (continued)**</u>

Cedric Jones - Boyfriend to Ada Grace James

Darryl Stephens - Lead Singer of the Soundbytes

Giangia Terry (Gigi) - Lead Singer of the Eight Faces of Eve

Helen Wilson-Singer in Eight Faces of Eve

Earlene Thomas - Singer in Eight Faces of Eve

Johnny Green - Childhood Friend of Lizzah and 1st Lead-Goldwings

Mark Edwards - 3rd Lead Goldwings

Solomon Oshanti - 2nd Lead Goldwings

Carmelita Evans - Lead Singer of The Georgettes

Bill Brady - Lead Singer of The Hearts of Gold

Robert Williams - Comedian and MC for Jamestown Summer Concert

<u>**Messengers**</u>

Gabriel - Arch Angel

Abaddon - Dark Angel

Malik (Angel) - Carries out God's commands for souls in Hell and Purgatory

Barciel (Angel) - Brings good news, Peace and blessings of God to all people

Sandelphon (Angel) - Protector of Unborn children

INTRODUCTION 1
TIME OF REFLECTION

As the sun set over the horizon, Milton Yarborough lay in what was once known as a safe house. Now, there was no place in Liverpool that had not suffered utter ruin. As he lay there, his life flashed before him. It wasn't until now that he seemed to see everything he did wrong in his life. Milton remembered being a small boy and how he loved to collect toy train cars. This thought brought a brief smile to his battered face. He uniquely designed and painted each car. He made so many of these cars that the train ran the length of the entire first floor of his home. He would often imagine that this train would bring his parents home, and they would take him to the theater to see this magical Mouse his classmates were always talking about.

As an adult, Milton had very little memory of his father, and he did not remember his mother at all. Odessa, his nanny, was careful to tell him all she knew about his parents and their mysterious disappearance. A few years back in 1938, a loving husband and wife, Melissa and John Yarborough, went to the theatre for a date night. Neither Melissa nor John was seen after that night. Odessa told him many stories about his parents' lives, what they liked to eat, and how they would dance and sing with each other. She said they were very kind to her family when they migrated from Belize. Odessa often spoke about how much they loved him and how happy they were to finally have a son.

Milton would tag along with Odessa when she visited her friends. They would dance and sing to the likes of Ella Fitzgerald, Duke Ellington, and Count Bassey. Odessa's best friend Jackie would come to town often. Everybody loved Jackie because she made them laugh. Everybody called her Moms for some strange reason I could never figure that out because she didn't have any children. People came from all over the world and paid a lot of money so that Moms could make them laugh.

Milton was always very sad about not knowing what happened to his parents. For years he fantasized about his mother. He thought he would come home from school one day, and Odessa would introduce him to the most beautiful woman in the world. He would then be told it was Melissa. He imagined her as a tall woman with coffee-brown hair, a milky white complexion, and hazel eyes. He pictured her with the most beautiful smile.

Milton loved the smell of lavender and thought his mom would likely smell like lavender perfume.

Odessa described his father as a stern businessman. He was tall with a stocky build. He had an olive complexion with extremely straight black hair. Odessa says I inherited my dark brown eyes from him. She says he had a high-pitched light voice that sounded deceptive, being the big man he was. His Dad and his friends would always fight and yell. He could vaguely remember sitting in his father's lap in the parlor. When the men came over, Odessa would take him for a nap or play with toys.

Once he became a young adult, Milton accepted that his parents were not likely alive, nor would they ever come back home. He looked through old news articles for answers about their disappearance. Milton could not find out much, and the few people who knew anything about that dreadful night were not talking. Milton was not getting any answers from anyone and he became very bitter. Milton decided never to love anyone because he didn't want to be hurt or deceived again. He devoted his life and chose a career investigating the mysterious disappearance of his parents. The problem was some people would rather he die than find out the truth.

There were many young women repeatedly trying to get Milton's attention, and there was none lovelier than young Annabelle. He thought she had the most beautiful brown eyes he had ever seen. Her copper-tone skin was smooth, and he was mesmerized by her smile. Besides Odessa, she was the only person who could make him feel a glimmer of hope or happiness. For hours they would walk and talk in the fields. He would often ask her to come to his quarters, where they would spend countless hours getting to know one another, laughing, and enjoying each other's company. Annabelle was a charming girl who could have easily captured his heart. He could not allow this to happen as he could not be distracted from his mission of finding and repaying the persons who murdered his parents. After seeing her well over six months, he refused her visits and decided never to see her again.

His reality came rushing back to him like flooding waters. Milton could not move his legs nor stand on his own anymore. He accepted this as fate, and he never bothered to call out for help. His own voice was but a whisper now and seemed so far away. The silence in his head screamed aloud as he remembered nothing but the pain of his past and at this moment, he regretted every decision he made in his lifetime. As he lay there in the darkness, he wondered how different his life would have been had he loved or even married Annabelle. Would he have made better decisions had he known and experienced the love of his parents? For thirty-three years, all he had wanted was to find them, get to know them, and find out what happened to them. Perhaps now his wait would finally be over. Before daybreak, Milton closed his eyes and drifted out of consciousness. The new day presented a sunrise that Milton Yarborough would never see.

INTRODUCTION 2
SECOND CHANCE GRANTED

INTRODUCTION 2

In some situations, second chances are few and far between, and some turn out even worse than the first. Milton came to awareness that he was in a grey and dreary place. He could see from the very beginning that Pergeau was not a happy place to be. People lay around moaning faintly while others screamed in pain. Everyone here was suffering. Milton began to feel a hint of physical pain himself. Watching others suffer made him sad, but he was not afraid.

He would soon realize there was no night or day on the Isle. No element of time existed here. There were no herbs nor trees of greenery. The Island of Pergeau, and everything in it, just was. The sun never came out, but it was never dark. The air was filled with a dense grey vapor that was always there. Intermittent fires would ignite and burn, but strangely, nothing was ever consumed by them. No water or flame retardant could put them out. As quickly as they started, they would go out and then start up someplace else. He thought that this must be what Odessa once described to him as Hell. Milton quickly dismissed that idea because these were small fires, not a large lake of fire. Something else was different about this place, as there were no infants or children. Souls could not sleep, nor was there any rest.

Nobody was eating, drinking, or making merry as people did on earth. Nobody thought about mating, dating, or marriage. They were souls, so there was no concern about appearance. There was no need for mirrors, as souls simply existed with no form. The only thing that was important to them was to keep away from the fires. After being in Pergeau for a while, Milton had been hurt repeatedly. He now understood the shrill cries of his fellow Souls as he himself was in severe pain. Despite his own discomfort, he helped the other ailing souls. He made spackle from the ash and rubbed it in the sores of the other ailing souls. Milton didn't know how much time had passed since coming to this dreadful place and he refused to accept this as his final fate. He had questions about Pergeau: What is this place? Why am I here? Nobody had the answers to his questions because all the other souls were in the same situation.

Milton heard rumors about a Meeting Place in The Structure where they could get help. His only hope was that this rumored Meeting Room really existed and that he would one day get to go in there. The Meeting Room was rumored to be in a big steel building. The building was said to be the only structure that existed on the Isle. His fellow Souls heard others describe it as a grey-like structure outside. Inside was rumored to be exquisitely dawned in gold fixtures and pearly white furnishings. The fires don't ignite or burn near it; neither is the vapor around the place, but it is full of bright, vivid light.

Some of the souls believe this structure is simply a mirage because no soul has ever found it on its own. Other souls describe it as being part of a parallel universe that can only be entered if sent for by God. Milton suffered much pain and was in agony. Every part of his form was in pain, but he still spackle-bandaged the other souls. He was doubtful that his questions would ever be answered but refused to accept this as his fate. He was in extreme pain. He felt drained and every part of his being was tired. He knew he could not find rest here.

Suddenly, the vapor cleared, and Milton found himself in the company of two of the tallest, most beautiful creatures imaginable. Their garments were a vivid white and deep blue. They were blinding, as Milton had not seen color in a very long time. He also noticed that now he no longer felt tired nor was he in any more pain. The one creature with a calm voice told Milton to "come." The Lord has heard your cries. Instantly, Milton found himself in a room with fixtures of gold, brass, and bright white furnishings, and the two creatures were with him. Barciel and Malik introduced themselves as messengers. God has heard your cries. He sees your compassion and how you desire to help others who are suffering, even when you are ailing yourself. Milton marveled at how beautiful and peaceful this place was. He was calmer now than he had been in a very long time.

Malik extended a welcoming stance, "I am Malik. I have a message for you from God. My assignment is to carry out God's will for the Souls that are in Hades". Barciel also extended a welcome to Milton, "I am Barciel. I am also a Messenger of the Father. My assignment is to do God's will and bring forth good news and blessings to the souls that are lost." Milton could not move. He was not afraid. He just could not move. Barciel continued, "You have questions about what this place is and why you had to come here. God has allowed us to give you the answers that you have been seeking."

INTRODUCTION 2

The Isle of Pergeau is a holding place for wandering and lost souls, "Your parents, Melissa and John, are with God. Melissa, your mother, has pleaded with God for mercy on your behalf. You were sent to Purgeau because you were rude and unloving to everyone while you were on Earth. Because things did not go your way, you chose to shut down and not accept the love that was abundantly given to you. Many people tried to love you, but you decided to render evil for all the good shown to you. You even took the very lives of two people. Did you think you would receive anything good after doing such evil things?"

Milton finally gained the ability to speak, "All I wanted was to be with my parents," Milton replied, "Everyone else I knew had their parents with them. I had to be raised by a hired servant. I did not think it was fair. When I found out who knew about my parents' disappearance, they told me nothing. They knew everything that happened to my parents and could have given me answers, but they wouldn't, so I killed them."

Barciel replied, with an angry, thunderous voice this time, "And you still know nothing!" Malik continued by saying, "Your parents are with God. They loved you while they were on the Earth, and they loved each other. Odessa was chosen and appointed by God to love and keep you. She is one of God's daughters, and she is a righteous person. Odessa still grieves about your demise every day. She blames herself for not being able to reach you. Your family knew that Odessa would carry out your parents' desires concerning you. Yes. They were unjustly killed. They were my people, and sometimes, I allow bad things to happen to good people if I choose to do so. On the other hand, you were justly killed by the family of the persons you intentionally murdered. The evil you have done was then rendered back to you."

You have, however, shown compassion since you've been placed here in Pergau. Because of this, God has heard your mother Melissa's plea. He has commanded us to give you another chance at life. "What do you want us to do for you?" Malik asked. "Do you want to enter eternal rest with us or return to the Earth for another assignment?" "I want to go to Earth," Milton said with enthusiasm. This time, I want to be filled with love and joy and to know what it is like to love and be loved in return. "Very well," Malik said, "You will have the capacity, but it will not come to you easily.

If you want to experience love and compassion, you will have to contend for it."

"Where on Earth would you like to go?" Barciel asked. "Milton replied that he wanted to return to the Earth as a woman like Odessa and her friends. A Negro woman who can sing and make music." "Why do you want to come back as such," asked Barchiel. "Because in all the Earth, I've found no lovelier or yet stronger creatures," Milton said. "They endure so much but still manage to succeed. Look at everything they have gone through. They have suffered from being enslaved, beaten, sold, and taken away from their families. My own father and grandfather used them to breed workers for our various plantations and mistreated them. We took them away from their men, raped them, and made them reproduce for people that didn't even recognize them as whole human beings. Some of their own men still abuse them, yet they still find the ability to love. They have the heart to forgive, and they thrive in the worst of circumstances. They still sing, and they dance, and raise up their children to love despite everything they've been through. Not only are they beautiful, but they also have an inner beauty and strength above any other creatures I've seen on Earth."

Malik smiled and said, "You are very observant, for these are indeed God's most beloved and gifted daughters. They are made most like him." After a long silence, Malik responded, "Very well," for God has given me permission to grant your desire. Know that this will be your last time going to Earth. This is your final chance to walk right and live right. Do not be selfish this time because God says that you have received his love freely, and he wants you to give it to others freely. Forgive others who hurt you just like God has forgiven you. You will have some hard times. But God will be with you always. If you fail on Earth this time to show love and compassion, the lake of fire awaits you.

Immediately, a very large window in the meeting room opened, and Milton saw a beautiful young maiden and an older gentleman. The young maiden was singing a lovely song, "This guy I Love." She had a soft and soothing voice that Milton thought surely brought rest to anyone who heard it. He thought this sweet young girl was indeed not singing to this older gentleman, as he looked old enough to be her father. As he studied the couple for a long while, another messenger appeared.

This was by far the most beautiful creature he had ever seen. His skin was flawless and the color of pure copper. He had long, coarse hair that was a rich brown color that glistened in the sunlight. His smile revealed a complete set of pearly, highly white teeth, and his demeanor was that of pure peace and rest. This messenger was clothed in a vivid peach and white garment and pure white sandals. His presence gave Milton an unexplainable peace.

"Come with me," he told Milton. "I am Sandelphon. My assignment is to keep and protect God's unborn children." Milton was so grateful that God was giving him another chance at life. He nodded to Malik and Barchiel as he basked in his newfound rest.

He followed Sandelphon to a resting place, and there, he slept. Milton was no longer in pain nor in any torment. He was now in perfect peace. He was with God, and he was safe in the master's arms.

Chapter One
This Guy I Love

HIRAM left very early for work in the morning. It had been a long night, as he and Esther were up late, arguing yet again. He could remember a time when they were so much in love. Hiram would rush home from work just to make dinner for her. She claimed that she loved everything he cooked. Truthfully, he really didn't cook all that great. Esther used to be front and center at all his concerts. Now, they barely attended Sunday Mass together. He knew in his heart there was nothing he could do to please this woman. Eventually, he just stopped trying. Hiram wished things were different between them. He believed if there had been a glimmer of hope for them, he would not be in such turmoil. Now, a divorce from his wife was just a matter of time. He was very tired, and the concert was in two days.

He knew the show would be a huge success because he and the cast had rehearsed the entire show four times earlier that day. Hiram had an incredibly gifted group of students this year. He believed this was his best-graduating class at the Conservatory ever. He knew the Dean would have no problem securing the funding needed to keep the school open, as the donors would be very well entertained.

Each night, sleep still managed to elude him. He had to do something about the longing he had for Towanna. Every day, he thought of nothing but her. Hiram never considered having an affair, especially not with any of his students. Towanna Graham, however, was no ordinary student. He first met her two years ago when she started his course on a probationary status. Dr. Graham asked him to take his daughter Towanna under his wing and perfect her voice. She wanted to audition for the musicals Porgy and Bess and Phantom of the Opera. Her father wanted to make sure she would be ready to grab the role. Hiram was not prepared for how lovely this young lady was, nor the talent she possessed. She was so refined and dainty, and her voice was just beautiful. This young girl had a range that was unbelievable. Not only was she an amazing singer, but she also played piano and guitar. She had a significant stage presence, and the ability to mesmerize the audience as she performed came from deep in her soul.

Towanna was also very peculiar. She had an innocent demeanor and was extremely shy for a young lady of sixteen years. That is until she got on the stage. She was a devout Catholic and never wore makeup, not even lipstick. She once told me that she considered joining the convent. She decided against it because she wanted to sing professionally. She also hoped to get married one day and have a few children.

Hiram never understood Towanna's fascination with vanilla flavor, but that's what she always smelled like. She said she liked the fragrance because it smelled pure and wholesome. To Hiram, she just always smelled like vanilla cookies. It was intriguing nonetheless and maybe this was part of what made her attractive. She spoke very eloquently and was very well-read. When she was not rehearsing or reading, she made extraordinary cloth dolls.

Hiram wondered if she ever thought of him or found him attractive. He was, after all, over fifteen years her senior. He found himself torn between doing the right thing of leaving her alone or pursuing her and following his heart. His concern was not for his marriage, as he could file for a divorce immediately. If he followed his heart, he stood to lose everything he had worked so hard for. His teaching career at the Conservatory would surely suffer. His friends and family would not understand. Still, he dreamed of Towanna every night. He wanted to know her and to please her in every possible way. Her father would certainly not approve, he thought. He would have no problem in providing for Towanna, but surely Dr. Graham would not want his only daughter with a man only five years younger than himself. Hiram had to have her, he thought to himself. He decided that he would pursue her. He would secretly send for her once the concert was over.

TOWANNA was very excited to be graduating from the most prestigious art college in Los Angeles. She had fought her father tooth and nail about going to The Music Conservatory. She wanted to study music on the local level in South Central, Los Angeles, but Dr. Ulysses Graham would not hear of it.

Everyone who knew her father knew that he always got what he wanted. This was especially true when it came to his only daughter, Towanna. When he wanted something from her, he always got it. She would never admit to him that he was right about his decision though. Her range was unbelievable now, and she was in command of her voice now more than ever.

Before attending the Music Conservatory, she had no desire to ever sing or perform in the Opera. She never could understand a word they were singing about and had a tough time following the story. Now, she will graduate in six months and has been cast in the lead role in Porgy and Bess. The rehearsals would tentatively start just three days following her graduation, and Towanna was so excited.

Dr. Graham was extremely protective of Towanna. After all, this was his only child, his baby daughter. He had wanted other children, but his wife had such a hard time after the birth of Towanna. After her death, he vowed to do everything he could to make his daughter successful and happy. It was amazing to him how much she favored her mother now.

After her death, Rose, Dr. Graham's sister, moved to the family home to help raise the child. Towanna had many questions about her mother, especially about that night when she was found unresponsive. Although her mother died over eleven years ago, Towanna remembered everything as if it had happened yesterday. Closing the chapter with things she could not understand, Towanna found her joy in music by singing and writing new lyrics. She spent hours listening to the radio and singing her favorite songs. When she was not in school, she helped her Aunt Rose in the bakery or spent hours making dolls. Towanna had very few friends that were her age. Most of her time was spent studying or rehearsing for recitals.

She thought all of the boys her age were very immature. All they did was hang out in the neighborhood park and drink silly soda. They never addressed her by name, nor did they ask her out. She was always "that yellow girl" or the Catholic kid. The girls her age made fun of her hair and clothes. They called her names like Plain Jane and Orphan Annie. Towanna often wondered why people were so cruel. It was something about Mr. Blandon that she found oddly attractive. She did not think he was a handsome man because, after all, he was old enough to be her father. Mr. Blandon was always nice to her. He often gave her good advice about some of the conflicts she had with other students. She was very much intrigued by the patience he had with her while going over her lessons.

After all, she thought to herself, she had him alone to thank for working with her voice. It was because of Mr. Blandon's persistence that she was chosen to star in Porgy and Bess, but it was deeper than just that. Towanna felt within her heart there was something deeper about him that she desired to explore.

The theater had once again been packed year for the annual fundraising concert. All the students were beaming with excitement about their success. The Dean of Admissions was happy because they raised a whopping twenty thousand dollars, and more donations were still coming in. Everyone was happy and wildly celebrating the success of the concert.

As Dr. Graham and Aunt Rose stood by waiting to take Towanna home, Hiram came by to shake their hand. Smiling from ear to ear, they complimented him on how much he had helped Towanna and thanked him for helping her obtain success. He assured the pair that Towanna was talented, and he merely brought out the gift that was already within her. As they continued to chat, Hiram decided that tonight would be the perfect time to approach Towanna. He told Dr. Graham about the after-social the cast was having and assured him that if he allowed her to attend, he would see Towanna getting home safely. After gaining their approval, Hiram went to his dressing room to make preparations for his potential guest.

As the last of the students were leaving, Towanna stood in the hallway waiting for Mr. Blandon to take her home. It was getting late, she thought. She was really surprised that her father had given his permission for her to stay and join the party. Towanna had a good time talking with her classmates. She felt extraordinarily lightheaded and free this evening. She thought maybe something was in the red juice she and her classmates were drinking. She was looking forward to getting together with them again very soon. Hiram came in the hallway and instructed Towanna to come to his dressing room for a moment.

Once inside, she was surprised at how well-furnished his dressing room was. The smaller rooms designated for the other cast members had only potato chips or pretzels with one soda per person. This room had real appetizers with red wine and chocolate-covered strawberries on the dressing table. It also had a private bathroom with a walk-in shower. This master dressing room also had a small piano so the leads could practice before going on stage. She thought maybe she would have this type of treatment waiting for her when she performed with Porgy and Bess.

The thought of her playing the lead role in this fantastic musical made her beam with excitement and joy. Towanna was about to live her dream and she was looking forward to every minute of it.

When Mr. Blandon emerged from the private bath, he was shirtless. Although she was a bit startled by this at first, she did not admit to him that it bothered her a bit, even when he asked. Towanna went to the piano and began to play and sing while she waited for him to finish getting dressed.

You're Amazing
This Guy I Love, The Only one for me
This Guy I Love, When I look in your eyes, I see
That you and I are meant to be
Together forever as You're the only one for me
Take me away from here, Chase away all my hurt and fears

Hiram stood behind her as she played. He watched her for quite a while. She was so engrossed in playing the music that she did not notice him watching her. He grabbed her around her waist and began kissing her on her cheek and then her neck. When she did not resist, he began to kiss her breast and continued down to her thigh. He embraced her with such tender care that although she was surprised, she could not resist. "Have you ever been kissed like this before?" he asked. "Yes. I mean, no, Mr. Blandon," she replied. He looked into her eyes and said, "Just for tonight, call me Hiram, okay?" She nodded her head in agreement.

They made sweet love over and over and played for over two hours. Hiram looked into her eyes and told her that he loved her and would never leave her. He explained that if anyone found out what had happened between them, he could lose everything he worked for. They agreed to keep their relationship a secret until after graduation. He promised they would be together soon after her graduation.

SIX MONTHS LATER

Towanna stood in the long procession to receive her diploma. Until now, she managed to keep her pregnancy a secret from Mr. Harvey, the Dean of Students, and that was certainly a miracle. Nobody, not even Dr. Grraham, knew who her baby's father was and she could never tell him. She felt sick and well, fat all the time. Towanna was surprised to see her father in the audience. He had been so disappointed when he found out about the baby that he vowed never to have anything else to do with her until she got rid of it. Auntie Rose must have given him a serious talking to, she thought to herself.

As she walked down the aisle, she saw Mr. Hiram Blandon. Seated next to him was a beautiful, refined, well-dressed older lady and they were holding hands. She knew at that point he would never come for her after graduation as he promised. A few days later, the producers of Porgy and Bess rescinded their offer to her. They said she could not play the lead role while she was with the child. It was now evident to Towanna that it was she who had lost everything that had been important to her. Towanna certainly could not think about any of this now. Her focus was on giving birth to a beautiful, healthy baby. Oh, how she looked forward to becoming a mother. She used to read and sing sweet songs to her bundle of joy each day. When she wasn't singing to the baby, she read stories. As much as she pleaded with her father to let her keep the child, Dr. Graham was not hearing any of this. Neither Towanna nor Aunt Rose were able to convince him otherwise. Towanna would never get to hold or even see her baby girl. Since the baby's birth, life for Towanna has never been the same.

She never had more children, nor did she marry. She longed to see her sweet little baby, which gave her so much joy for nine months, but it did not happen.

The years ahead for Towanna were filled with many challenges, some disappointments, and great success. Through the years, she played in many films and produced a plethora of songs. The world still sings and enjoys many of these songs today.

CHAPTER TWO
AN ANSWERED PRAYER

Isn't it wonderful when things you have longed and prayed for are brought to pass? Robin and Henry Atkins were overjoyed. They had finally received the call from Holy Family Center and been given the go-ahead to start adoption proceedings. They tried for many years to have children, but it did not happen. They would now be able to share the love they felt for each other with their very own child. They have been doing well since they moved from Chicago to Los Angeles. The only thing that was missing was a child.

Lizzah Doreen Atkins (Lizzah) was a beautiful baby. She was the color of smooth cocoa with big, beautiful, bright eyes. She had a thick, full head of long hair. That was very rare for a little baby of only six weeks old. Each time she smiled a piece of their hearts melted. Lizzah stole a piece of their hearts each day. Robin doted on her and dressed her in white dresses every day. Her friends Margaret and Louris would come over with toys and even more clothes and every minute, Lizzah was Kodak ready.

Robin changed Lizzah's dresses every two hours. Although Henry thought Robin was being a bit excessive, he said nothing to her of this. Henry got joy out of just seeing her happy. He was happy also, for the most part. He had great disdain for his job and did not see any opportunities to grow in his company. His hours at the lighting company were often cut short as people were not ordering custom chandeliers as much as they used to. His own Venetian Blind business was thriving, and he was gaining many more customers. He often worked late hours just to fill the new orders that were coming in. He missed his life in Chicago and felt there were more opportunities and better employment there. He hated not being able to go to the tavern that he and his brothers owned there. He was just so far away from the rest of his family. Robin loved Los Angeles, though, and she did not want to leave. He was now a new and proud father and Lizzah had apparently stolen his heart. This was his baby daughter. He would love and protect her with everything he had. They would, however, leave Los Angeles sooner than they both imagined.

Robin noticed that her baby was nervous when hearing sudden shrill, loud noises. Lizzah was terrified whenever hearing the Chicago fire trucks or an ambulance. The only thing that would comfort her was Robin or Henry's voice or the sound of music. It could be any type of music. Just like Henry,

Lizzah loved music. As an infant, she spent hours with Henry when he played records.

As a small child, Lizzah's imagination was fully activated when she listened to music. She protested when it was bed or nap time as little Lizzah could listen to music all day and all night. She decided she would try to make her voice do what the people on the records did. At first, her parents would laugh. They then noticed how sweet her voice was and how happy she was when she was singing. Robin and Henry recognized Lizzah's rare talent and wanted to help her develop it. As a young child, Lizzah would sing all day and every day. She woke up and went to bed, singing. Lizzah even attempted to eat and sing at the same time until Henry put his foot down. She sang on the radio and in every television commercial. The only way Robin got away from Lizzah singing was to go to the bathroom. If Robin stayed in there too long, Lizzah sat outside the bathroom door and serenaded her there. Robin and Henry decided to give Lizzah all the tools to become successful in music. After all, Robin thought it was high time that this child serenade somebody else for a change. Lizzah Doreen Atkins did not miss a beat in doing just that.

Chapter Three
Who Am I

One who has a gifted child should make sure those talents are well developed. Children must always be encouraged to exercise their imagination, and Robin and Henry did just that. Because Lizzah loved the arts and was still singing and dancing, Robin was determined to get her known to the rest of the world.

Robin wanted Lizzah to go to the Music Conservatory in Chicago, IL, but Henry would not allow it. He said they could not afford it. Robin stumbled across a modeling ad for infants and children and decided that she would take Lizzah to try it out. Lizzah was cast within 15 minutes of the interview and Robin was instructed to bring her back camera ready in just two days. She also had to bring with her ten outfits in three different categories: playtime, naptime and Sunday best. Robin enjoyed making clothes. Lizzah would go on to model for 4-5 years throughout Chicago and the suburbs. She loved meeting new people and all of the attention she received.

In addition to modeling, Robin enrolled Lizzah in Ms. Pat's school of dance, where she learned ballet and modern dance. She would perform with the dance school at places like Drury Lane Theatre and the Civic Opera House for the next seven years. Lizzah delivered her first solo performance at eight years old singing the Disney tune Some Day My Prince Will Come.

The dance school opened opportunities for Lizzah to audition for various plays and TV shows, and Lizzah stole the show in every role she played. She excelled in modern dance but was not able to master ballet because her ankles were too weak. Despite her success in acting, modeling and dancing, Lizzah's passion was singing. When the music auditions didn't happen in her favor, she became discouraged. Once she became a pre-teen, the acting roles stopped because people were looking for babies, not older children. Ms. Pat suddenly became ill and passed away, so the dance school closed.

Lizzah had a hard time adjusting to the changes and getting along with her classmates. Her grades were above average, but she began to hate school. Lizzah had three good friends: Stephany, Renea, and Britt. Although the three of them were thick as thieves and did everything together, Lizzah often found herself feeling overwhelmed with sadness. She was often irritable and music was the only thing that made her feel content. In the evenings and after dinner, homework and chores were complete, Lizzah listened to WVON radio until bedtime. Each day she picked new songs to sing. She loved talented artists like Mini Riperton, Diana Ross and later, Donna Summer. She decided that she would start her own group. Lizzah and her friends rehearsed a plethora of songs. And one year later, Lizzah and The Wonderettes did their first school talent show. They had no harmony and no band. They sounded horrible, but for Lizzah, it was only the beginning.

Chapter Four
Humble Beginnings

Although Lizzah was an above-average student, she absolutely hated school because it had become very stressful. Most of her classmates did not know she existed, and frankly Lizzah was not very friendly. As far back as she could remember, all Lizzah wanted to do was to sing. Now, she was not on TV, dancing or modeling anymore. Lizzah was teased about her weight and her dialect. Others talked about her knocked knees or her acne. Some of her classmates laughed at her because Robin still made most of her clothes. Lizzah loved most of the clothes Robin made for her because none of her friends wore clothes that were like hers. She thought Robin was a great fashion designer. She also loved mostly everything her mother cooked.

Holidays were a big thing in Robin and Henry's house. Robin and many of Lizzah's aunts spent days preparing dinner. Everyone would eat, spin records, and have a great time. Sometimes Henry asked Robin to make a lot of weird food like hog head cheese, salt pork and brains and eggs. If Lizzah had overnight guests from school, Robin was certainly going to introduce them to the traditional Sunday breakfast of brains and eggs. Lizzah and her family would then be known around school as "the brain eaters."

Adolescence had presented Lizzah with many emotional challenges. As a result, the only time she was ever happy was when listening to music. Music and Singing Lizzah opened a whole new world for Lizzah and music would later become one of the most important aspects of her life. Ada Grace James was the person to talk to when young groups wanted to get into local entertainment. She graduated from Water South High School a few years back and had a lot of connections in the Teen Arena. After a pretty hard life on the streets of Chicago, it was determined that her father was none other than Stephan James, the founder of Jamestown Records. She was the "go to" person when it came down to getting your groups heard because she was a direct connection to the popular radio stations. Getting a group audition with her was almost impossible. Once you got in, you only got one shot to impress her. If she liked your performance, your group's life would change for the better immediately. The problem for Lizzah was she rarely, if ever, promoted any solo artist. Ada Grace had connections for opportunities in Chicago and Detroit. Her Father set her up with her own branch of his company and called it Talent Now. Ada Grace set up her business in the garage of her house in Englewood. If she does not like your performance, however, prepare to work a lot harder to get yourself known in the Teen-arena. She was not going to waste time on anyone or anything that was less than what she thought was perfection. Lizzah heard of Ada Grace through a mutual friend of hers, Johnny. He was the lead singer of a group called The Sifters. Johnny and Lizzah had performed together at many school talent shows and were very well received. Johnny often talked about his audition with Ada Grace and how she picked apart every bit of his performance. She said Johnny's group sounded good, but they all had two left feet. As hard as he tried, he could not dance and sing at the same time. This, Ada Grace said, was what was needed. She then had her Assistant show them the quickest way to the street.

Lizzah did not connect with Ada Grace to promote The Wonderettes. She decided to find another way to fine-tune the Wonderettes and take them to the next level. At present, she and Johnny are doing quite well working together. They had a lot of requests to perform the song "Only Your Love." And they had become popular for a little while doing talent shows.

As for the Wonderettes, rehearsal was always a challenge. Stevetta's parents would never let her out of their sight to rehearse. Briitt's mother always had her doing one hundred and one chores around the house, and according to her mom, they were never quite right. She could never come to any rehearsal unless she slipped out of the house. Robin and Henry were always open to them rehearsing at the house and willing to endure the noise. The only time they refused is when Lizzah would get a sassy mouth and then Robin would say no as a punishment. It was oh so rare to get all three young ladies in rehearsal at the same time. Because of this, when Lizzah and Johnny were not performing together, she performed by herself.

Finding a band was another challenge for the Wonderettes. There was an organ player at the church who only played church music. Lizzah had no interest in church music because she thought it was strange. She thought about joining a church choir only to help strengthen her voice. She didn't do it because everybody she knew who went to church stayed all day long.

She decided that one hour in the Catholic Church would be just fine with her.

There were also the "bad boys" at Jackson High School, and they could play really well. They always hung around the school singing and harmonizing and talking to the senior girls. Everyone at Jackson High knew them, but nobody ever saw them go inside the school. There was Eddie Ray, who played lead guitar; TJ was on the keyboard, and Rodney was on drums. These guys were "The Band," which was in high demand and played for a lot of groups.

Lizzah thought Eddie Ray was really cute, but he never talked to anybody. Most of the time, he just starred in space. Eddie Ray only came to life when he would sing or play the guitar. Many of the girls were really infatuated with him, but nobody could get close to him. If he wasn't singing and playing, he never acknowledged anybody's presence.

Rodney and TJ had many girlfriends. They were not cute, but they had status with all the girls because they were "The Band." Lizzah dismissed any idea of getting The Band or the Wonderettes to help her. After all, they were in high school and all the Wonderettes were in catholic grammar school. Stephany's father still picked her up from school every day. There was no way to sneak off or talk to them. Robin would have a fit and let's not even think about what Henry would do. She went past Jackson High every day after school just to watch the band talk, play and harmonize. She had to figure out a way to talk to TJ. She had to get him to notice her.

Chapter Five
Lizzah Rebels

Corrine Palmer was a Freshman at St. Joseph High School. Lizzah met her a few months prior at a recruitment seminar for new students, and the freshman students were not in uniform that day. Lizzah would start as a Freshman at St. Joseph's in the fall of the year. The challenge was to keep her out of trouble until she could graduate. Lizzah and Corrine wore the same size. Corrine's mom let her wear anything she wanted it seems, and as a result, Corrine dressed and looked like she was about 25 years old. Lizzah thought Corrine dressed nicely, and she was interested in creating a new look for herself. She and Robin began to shop for age-appropriate styles, but they barely agreed on anything. Lizzah liked hot pants and halter tops, but Robin would not allow it at first. Lizzah was forced to recreate outfits from scraps of clothes she already had. Corrine gave her a few blue jean pants and tops, and it wasn't long before Lizzah had a small hidden wardrobe she would merely wear to get TJ's attention. Robin noticed that Lizzah had begun to come home late from school every day. She knew her daughter was lying because the excuses late just seemed to get completely crazy. She had heard them all, from "I got on the wrong bus" to "The teacher made us stay to clean the classroom." This was the part Robin began to dread more than anything. She and Henry had a stranger in their own house now. Oh, how she missed her beautiful little baby girl as she did not know who this new person was. Lizzah no longer ran to greet Henry with Hugs and kisses when he came home from work. She was either closed off in her room or just not there.

Robin knew some of her challenges and was very concerned because Lizzah was always angry or sad. She had no idea how to help her get through this thing called puberty. They did not even like this child at this point and they had to remember that Lizzah was theirs. They would love her no matter what. Robin did know that it was time she found out just what Ms. Lizzah was up to, and she intended to do it quickly.

It was finally getting warm outside, and Lizzah was finding it hard to sneak past Sister Brunod to get back to school after dismissal. Every day, she stood at the door long after school was over, doing heel-toe exercises and watching for anything suspicious. After 20 minutes or so, she would finally go back to the school and go to the office to finish up her paperwork. Lizzah would then return to the school, go into the tunnel, and change her clothes. She did this every day just to walk past TJ. This time Lizzah had on a bellbottom seersucker suit with a matching halter top. The outfit was not revealing originally, but Corrine had taught Lizzah how to roll and fold the top, showing just about everything. This would undoubtedly get TJ's attention, she thought. Lizzah had taken extra care in putting on her makeup too. Even her eyebrows had wings and were shaded perfectly, she thought. Maybe he will say something to her today, and she can ask him about playing for the Wonderettes.

After School Hours

When Lizzah emerged from the school tunnel there was no trace of the catholic school uniform she wore earlier that morning. She was moving so fast that she did not see Sister Brunod standing in the side door as she passed. Lizzah was off to meet the Johnson twins. Every day, she walked with them, going toward their home, passing Jackson High. Today will be the day that she will talk to TJ, she said to herself. If he does not notice her today, she would just have to approach him.

Sis. Brunod stared out the window in utter disbelief. She had to put an end to this once and for all. Never had she seen any of their students sneak back into the school. This child was not only creeping back into the school but was emerging from our school with scantily dressed clothing. She would have to call Mrs. Adkins immediately.

Jackson High

TJ stood in front of Jackson High. He usually had a group of girls around him, but today, it was just him and Rodney in front of the school. They seemed to be discussing something important. She started to walk past him yet again but decided that the introduction would happen now or not at all. "Excuse me," she said. "Aren't you TJ from the Band?" "Yeah." "Who you?" said TJ. "I'm Lizzah. I see you all the time. I heard a lot about the Band. I want to know if you can play and work with my group." "I know who you are," said TJ. "You that little girl that sing with Johnny sometime. And why you walk by here errday wit da Twins and don't say nothing?" "You're always busy," Lizzah said. Giggling and smiling at the same time.

Out of nowhere, Robin pulled up and grabbed her. Lizzah Dorina Adkins. "What are you wearing? Why aren't you not at home an hour and a half after school has dismissed? Get in the car," Robin demanded. TJ smiled. "Don't worry," he said. "Maybe I'll get to hear your group after the summer break is over. You'll be off punishment by then," Rodney and TJ just laughed, but Lizzah did not see anything funny about being humiliated. Once they were home, Lizzah retreated to her room for the rest of the day. She didn't even join Robin or Henry for dinner. She didn't even care about not having dessert on that day.

Chapter Six
Opportunity Knocks

Timothy Jonnigan (TJ) was living his dream. He was seventeen years old, and already, his career was taking off to a level he had never imagined. The Band was booked every weekend for the next six months, and he had little time to do anything but rehearse. He dropped the last three classes that he signed up for at Jackson High. Although he hung out for a while at the school every day, he had yet to go inside. Everyone just assumed he was a student because he was in front of the school every day.

When his mother found out that he never went to school, she made him leave her house. He could not get her to understand that he was living large and did not need a high school or college diploma. Although he was no longer living at home with his mother, he still paid all her utilities and some other bills every month. She didn't like what he was doing, but she never turned down the almighty dollar, he thought to himself. Now, he had his apartment, a brand-new car, and a different girl every week.

His Band was well on their way, and they were in high demand. Aside from the band profits, business was great. He had a lot of repeat customers, and they were spreading the news about how good his merchandise was. He had clientele in Illinois, Indiana and now, Wisconsin.

Even though business was great, making beautiful music was TJ's passion. All he ever wanted to do was play and sing. He was not comfortable risking his life nor being in danger of going to jail every day, but business was booming, and he was making a lot of tax-free money.

It was becoming very clear to him that he would have to eventually find a backup, or even a replacement, for Eddie Ray. Eddie Ray played lead guitar. He sang and rocked a harmonica simultaneously. He was an essential part of the group. It was safe to say without him, their sound would not be the same. He was the most popular of them all, but he was getting high too much and dipping hard into the inventory. It was becoming a two-hour process sobering him up just to perform. His brother Derrick had warned him that Eddie Ray was weak and that he was using. He would have to find a way to get him back sober so the Band would not lose its popularity.

TJ loved the ladies, and the ladies loved TJ. He didn't have any special one that he liked over the other; he enjoyed them all. The idea of losing any one of his girls was extremely upsetting to him. That is until he met the lovely young Lizzah. He could not understand what his fascination was with this little girl, as she was only about 14 years old. Maybe it was the fact that she was trying so hard to be a grown-up, but she was really an innocent child. She first approached TJ in front of Jackson High about working with her group. She and Johnny had done a few duets together, and they sounded good. Lizzah had a nice sound, and TJ thought they could make beautiful music together one day in more ways than one. She is so young, and TJ was not trying to have confrontations with anybody's parents, as he was already at odds with his own mother. He had many women, and he did not have to deal with any drama.

Still, he thought of her every day, sometimes all day. He certainly did not even consider the offer to work with her and the little group, but he hoped he would have the chance to work with her alone one day.

TJ's wish came true about two years later when his band played for St. Rita's Music Department fundraiser. He had not wanted to take the gig at first, but they really needed the work. There were twenty-three different performers from eight different schools that were cast in the show. None of them captured his attention like Liizzah. As they rehearsed, he wondered if she knew who he was and was just playing it off because her mother embarrassed her so badly that day in front of Jackson High School. He thought she had such a beautiful voice and she was a lot more grown up now, almost legal. He knew she would do much better as a solo artist and he was glad she was no longer singing with the other girls.

Lizzah performed two songs. One was by the well-known artist Minnie Riperton, "Loving You," and the other was by the Late Blues singer Billie Holiday.

The Music Department had selected this number and Lizzah had been chosen to sing "Strange Fruit", but she hated the song. It was such a challenge for Lizzah because she had a hard time getting into the lyrics and did not know what the song meant. To her, it was just a long, slow, and boring song. TJ gave her a brief history lesson about Billie Holiday and the meaning behind the song. When she learned that the song was about the lynching and civil injustices that Black people once endured in the South, she performed with great passion. Oddly enough, this was the performance that got Lizzah the most compliments and was most enjoyed by all. After this night, Lizzah was requested to perform during many shows. She was also repeatedly called upon to sing The National Anthem at many of the school games. After the show, there was a big celebration at Club Trinidad, and all the performers were allowed to attend. Lizzah and her friends Corrine and Britt were there, along with some other aspiring artists. She thanked TJ for helping her with one of the most challenging songs she ever had to sing. All of the girls who liked TJ were watching as Lizzah left Club Trinidad. TJ ran out of the club hoping to catch up to Lizzah, but she was gone.

Chapter Seven
ALL ABOUT ME

Lizzah had a great time during the summer after graduation. She experienced a lot of new and exciting things that year. Robin took her to Los Angeles for four weeks, and on the plane ride, Robin and Lizzah were treated like royalty. To Lizzah it was not like any of the other plane rides she had taken before. Lizzah had free reign to go from one side of the aircraft to the other, and the seats were comfortable and roomy. They had plenty of room and plenty of food that was good. Except for another elderly couple, she and Robin were the only people to occupy that section of the plane.

Robin introduced Lizzah to all the friends she had made in LA before she and Henry moved back to Chicago. There was Mrs. Margaret, the Executive Secretary to a wealthy Jewish lawyer. Lizzah loved to go to her house because she had a swimming pool in her backyard and her son Rudy had a lot of friends that would come over. There was also Mrs. Heard and her husband, an elderly couple whom Robin knew well. Robin said Mr. and Mrs. Heard were Robin's godparents. They lived in South-Central LA. They did not have a swimming pool, so Lizzah went outside and made friends with people in the neighborhood. She joined with a group of teens and won second place in a pop-up talent show.

Lizzah finally met her Godparents, Bob and Louris, and To Lizzah, Ms. Louris was so cool. Although she was a strict disciplinarian and a no-nonsense person, Lizzah loved and respected her immediately. Louris told Lizzah they would get along fine but never to lie to her about anything. It was important to Lizzah to get along with Louris. She was the first adult who was able to convince Robin to let her get her ears pierced and wear makeup. Robin had put a stop to any form of makeup after that day in front of Jackson High School.

Lizzah loved California, and she especially loved her godparents and, she loved their house. The house had two huge white pillars on each side of the front porch that reminded her of the White House. In the backyard were two enormous peach trees that yielded the sweetest peaches she had ever tasted. On the other side of the yard was a bunch of mint leaves and Perrnials. Everyone loved to put the mint leaves in their iced tea instead of sugar.

Bob and Louri's daughter Denise was the coolest person Lizzah had ever met. Although Denise was four years older than Lizzah, they got along well. She had a lot of friends who were children of singers and movie stars, and for two weekends straight, they did nothing but go to parties. Lizzah just could not contain her excitement because there were no chaperones at these parties. They were free to do whatever they wanted for as long as they wanted. There was plenty of food and trays of pink and blue cigarettes for everyone. None of the adults came to see what they were doing. This was all so new and like a dream come true for Lizzah.

She was so tempted to join in the fun but remembered the promise she made to her parents. She promised Robin and Henry that she would never take drugs or smoke any kind of marijuana. Robin and Lizzah explored the entire city of Los Angeles. They drove to the hills to see the Hollywood sign and then along Rodeo Drive. On another day, they went to a movie and saw a Tina Turner concert. Later that evening they stopped at the Carnation Plant for Ice cream. They went to Disney Land, and Robin bought Lizzah everything she wanted. This had been the best vacation ever, Lizzah thought to herself. She had two questions for Robin: why did they ever leave Los Angeles? Do they really have to go back to Chicago? Two days before they were to come back to Chicago, Denise called Robin with some sad news.

Louris and Bob were at a party the night before. Louris suffered a heart attack and died instantly. Robin delayed flying back to Chicago to help Bob with funeral arrangements. Lizzah was heartbroken yet thankful that she got a chance to meet her godmother before she died. It also made her wonder briefly about her birth parents. She longed to know them and what type of people they were. Did she look like her mother or her father and why, oh why, did they not want her? Robin told Lizzah everything she had learned about her birth parents through the adoption agency. Looking at the adoption papers, Lizzah learned that her mother was a student at the Conservatory of Los Angeles and her father was her mother's teacher. Robin assured Lizzah that she loved her and that she would do anything to help her find her birth parents.

Lizzah loved her mother also and felt terrible for being so rebellious at times. There were so many things about herself that Lizzah did not yet understand. She thought to herself that she would have to move back to Los Angeles to get the answers to her questions. She longed to try smoking this marijuana everyone was talking about. Lizzah thought if she were to try smoking marijuana, she might not feel sad every day. One thing was for sure: she would have to be more focused on her music career. It simply had to be done, and nobody knew how important it was for her to accomplish this.

Freshman year was a fascinating start for Lizzah because she met a lot of new friends. She also got a lot of singing engagements. Her classes were hard for her to grasp, especially algebra. She still hated school and only went because Robin told her she had to go. Corrine introduced Lizzah to her friends Liz and Cocoa. They were Juniors, and they loved to go to parties. Their parents worked all the time, even on the weekends. Lizzah never ever came straight home from school. She had no concept of how worried Robin was about her and punishments did not matter. As soon as she went back to school, she would do the same thing all over again. Liz and Cocoa were distant cousins to the famous Reggie and the Family Malone. They were busy working on a new single, Electric Love, and they expected the song to top the charts. A year later, it did. As a result, they rehearsed and performed non-stop. Lizzah spent a lot of after-school hours in the Malone Family rehearsals.

As a rule, Reggie never allowed outsiders in rehearsals, but he made an exception because Lizzah always came with his little cousins. When Reggie saw how interested Lizzah was in the group, he began to use her.

She would be asked to go get water and beer and even to roll their cigarettes. Her mother did not know where Lizzah was, and she could never tell her. The Malones began to use Lizzah and Cocoa as backup background singers on the few occasions that his sisters were not available.

Lizzah would tell Robin she was at a friend's house spending the night, but in reality, she would be performing at clubs. Up until this point, Lizzah upheld the promise she made to her parents never to use marijuana although everyone she knew was smoking. She was becoming more curious each day.

During the last half of Freshman year, Lizzah performed every Friday and some Saturdays for six months straight. Because of her brief backup stints with the Malones, she was called on to perform at many schools and charitable events, games, and, unknown to the adults, some clubs. Her grades were so low that even she was surprised when she passed all her classes. The school was not a priority to her, and she barely did enough to get by. Robin tried to keep up with her, but it was pretty much impossible.

Lizzah was chosen as one of twelve students to perform at St. Joseph's annual March Ball. This fundraiser was necessary because the donations received from the event were a deciding factor in the cost of tuition the following year. Robin and Henry were tired of paying high tuition for Lizzah's mediocre grades.

This was their chance to support the fundraiser, surprise Lizzah, and see her performance. As Robin and Henry sat in the audience, they were very proud of their daughter's accomplishments. Her voice was clear as a bell and was the strongest they had ever heard. At the end of the performance, Henry greeted Lizzah with a half dozen red roses, and Lizzah was speechless. She was surprised and happy to see them both. After the show, Lizzah introduced her parents to some of her friends.

As Robin and Henry were talking with teachers and friends, Lizzah excused herself to go to the lady's room. The bathroom on the auditorium side of the school was never ever monitored by school staff. It was always the place where young ladies went to smoke weed and cigarettes and tonight was not an exception. While in the bathroom, Corrine asked Lizzah to help her fix her ripped blouse. When Lizzah did not return to the auditorium right away, Robin went looking for her. She came through a crowd of girls puffing on pink and blue cigarettes and found Lizzah and Corrine amid the smoke.

Although up until that point, Lizzah had never even attempted to smoke even a cigarette, Robin angrily accused her of breaking her promise to them. Lizzah begged and pleaded with her mother to believe that she had not done anything wrong, but Robin did not believe her. She even told Henry, and they both accused her of being a "stupid dope head." She was grounded for two weeks and not able to go out and perform.

Lizzah was very hurt and angry that Robin did not believe her. She was especially upset, as her father was disappointed with her for something she had not even done. For two weeks after school, Lizzah came straight home, slammed her room door shut and stayed in there. Once her punishment was over, she performed with Johnny at the Metro Pub. He knew Lizzah was upset about something because she poured her passion into the performance like never before. The audience went wild that night as Lizzah performed. After the show, Johnny treated everyone to a party with smokes and Hopingaitors at his mother's house.

Before tonight, Lizzah would always just watch them and joke around with them while they got high. He was surprised to see that Lizzah joined right in. He was concerned and asked her if she was sure about not only smoking for the first time but mixing it with alcohol. He said he thought it was a bad idea. Lizzah insisted she was going to do it. Lizzah mumbled under her breath that she had been accused of it and had not done anything wrong. Now she was doing it.

Lizzah sat on the couch in Johnny's mother's house. At that moment, she was not angry with anyone. She did not feel sad or hurt anymore. She felt like everyone and everything was just far, far away. In a way, she felt free, but she was also exhausted and very hungry. This will never do she thought to herself because the little cigarette had taken away her ability to walk properly. How can anyone perform in this state of mind, she thought to herself. Lizzah came home late again, as usual. She was so high that she did not notice Robin on the stairs watching her when she came in. She went straight to her room and passed out across her bed. Robin knew in her heart then that Lizzah was telling the truth because the little haint that had just come into her house was not the daughter she knew even two weeks ago. Robin was afraid, and she now had a reason to be. What had she done, she thought to herself, and what would she do now?

Chapter Eight
Lizzah and TJ

It had been a long time since Lizzah was able to sing close to her house. Most of her performances were on the near North or West side of Chicago. Club Rapture was a favorite hang-out spot for teens and young adults in Chathamsville, and Lizzah was really excited to be performing there. She did not want to disappoint her parents and smoke again, but her nerves were shot. She stopped in the club lounge so she could take just two pulls off the joint she bought on her way there. She was afraid that if she smoked anymore, it would affect her performance.

Until tonight, she had managed to avoid TJ and the band. Lizzah did think he knew who she was when he coached her a while back. She always remembered the look on TJ's face back at Jackson High School. She hoped and prayed that he didn't remember her or the bizarre incident. The club was packed; they were turning people away before the show even began. The show participants and the band got a chance to rehearse and Lizzah was to perform the opening song, Sweet and Sexy Stranger, while doing a tastefully provocative tap dance at the same time.

Singing, for Lizzah, was never a problem, but dancing and singing simultaneously made her extremely nervous. As a child, even Henry had given up on teaching her how to dance. She had improved a lot after being in the dance studio, but to her, like Johnny, she still had two left feet. With just two pulls of the weed, the fear and anxiety went away, and she thought her coordination improved immediately. She was mellow for a change and focused.

Lizzah put her heart and soul into her songs that night, and the crowd enjoyed her very much. Her performance surprised the band and the club owners, and even Lizzah was surprised in herself. It always felt extremely good to her when she was well received, she thought to herself.

The last number Lizzah was to perform was at the end of the show. It was a melody of three songs: You've Got a Friend, Lean on Me and closing with the Gospel song Precious Lord Take My Hand. It was so strange to her to have to sing a gospel song in the club, but surprisingly to her, everyone was touched by it. She didn't quite understand what all the lyrics of the song meant or what had just happened. She just closed her eyes and began to sing. When she opened her eyes, everyone was crying and wiping their eyes. She didn't know if it was the two pulls from the weed or what was happening, but at that moment, she felt content, like the words in the song had a certain type of power. One day, she would have to find out what the lyrics of this song meant, she thought to herself.

After the show, TJ and Eddie Ray were standing in front of the club. Eddie Ray was joking around and had all of them laughing. Lizzah was surprised because Eddie Ray never talked to anyone. She smiled at the two of them as she walked past, saying goodnight to them. TJ told her how much he liked her performance, and she thanked him. A minute later, TJ caught up to her, saying, "Hey, you got a minute?" She told him yes. "I just got to ask you one question," said TJ. "Okay," Lizzah says. "What do you want to know?" "You off punishment yet." "Oh, so you do remember," Lizzah said, laughing nervously.

TJ told her that he not only remembered the incident but also recognized her and how she and Johnny always performed together. He said he had hoped to run into her ever since that day.

Lizzah sat in TJ's car, and they laughed and talked for hours. They talked about everything from school and their parents. TJ told her of his passion for music and how he wanted to travel and do tours. He was open and honest to her about how he made his real money. The day after Mass, she and TJ met at a local club and diner, The Brass Monkey, and had dinner. Again, they talked for hours, and from that day forward, Lizzah and TJ were pretty much joined at the hip.

Lizzah was extremely fascinated by TJ's lifestyle. Although she knew a lot of ladies were interested in TJ, he never looked at any of them when they were together. It was like he only had eyes for her. TJ became very protective of Lizzah, and they spent a lot of time together.

Lizzah had not met anyone who had their own place before. She often told Robin she was spending the night at a friend's house, but she was really spending nights with TJ. Although she loved spending time there, she never entertained the idea of living with him because he always had people coming and going all hours of the night. Often, he helped her with homework and took her to and from school. When she was not singing, or he was playing or performing with the band, they were together.

Lizzah's relationship with her parents was not good. Robin tried hard to keep up with Lizzah but never really knew where she was or when she would come home. Henry repeatedly tried to put her on punishment, but it didn't work. As soon as Lizzah got out to go to school, she was as good as gone. The only thing that would make Lizzah come home after school is when Henry threatens to put her out of the house. Lizzah continued to do only enough schoolwork to get by. Many times she cut classes sitting right in the school lunchroom when she arrived late for class. Other times she went to the abandoned side of the school to smoke or drink beer. Although her career was getting off to a great start, she continued to feel sad and anxious about almost everything. She was in love with TJ. Three girls had tried to fight her about TJ just last week. She was so glad her friend Corrine had come to her rescue. Nobody, in their right mind, ever messed with Corrine. Robin and Henry wanted to meet TJ, but how would she introduce him was the question. Hi Mom, Dad this is TJ, my boyfriend. He plays in the band, and oh, he's also a drug dealer. Lizzah loved marijuana and now, she was drinking and smoking menthol cigarettes. Through it all, her performances improved, and she was in more demand than ever before. Although she was more interested in trying the Hash and Angel Dust, TJ would never allow it. He always made sure she only smoked and that what he gave her was safe.

Soon, Lizzah and TJ were doing a lot of shows together. They would revive and write a lot of love songs. TJ wrote a duet with Lizzah and called it "Only Your Love." They went over it a few times, and the crowd loved it the first time they performed the song.

She was so in love with TJ, and she hoped that one day he would make her his wife. After all, he was just in the drug business temporarily so he could pay his bills, right? She knew the day would come when the music would be enough, and he would not need to be in business to make ends meet. Lizzah was confident that she and TJ's future would be very bright. At this moment, she felt happy and content.

The next day, she joined Robin and Henry at St. Dorothy for family mass. Later, she went by TJ's house, and they went to see a movie. They came home early and didn't smoke but ordered a takeout pizza with a lot of weird toppings. TJ gave Lizzah a big glass of Hopingator while they listened to Dolemite. Lizzah did not understand Dolemite and to her, it was repulsive. Must be a guy thing, she thought to herself.

She noticed that TJ was not being himself. He was edgy and seemed nervous about something. He got a phone call and went out of the room twice to talk in private. This was not like him because they talked about everything. After the call ended, TJ grabbed Lizzah and kissed her for a very long time. Then he looked into her eyes and said, "I love you, my wife." He also told her that regardless of what happened to him in the future, he would never forget the times they spent together. This made Lizzah feel sad because TJ seemed to indicate that he was leaving her. He told her always to remember the words in the song he wrote for her and that he meant them from his heart. As he drove her home later that night, he encouraged her to be more diligent in her schoolwork. He said one of them had to complete school and that right now, it didn't look like he would be the one to do it.

Lizzah had no idea why he felt he could not go back to school if he wanted to. He promised to pick her up from school the next day so they could work on the songs for next week's show. He gave her another long kiss goodnight and watched her as she went into her house.

The next morning was a school day, and Lizzah was dragging around getting dressed as usual. Robin and Henry were both looking at the morning news and going on and on about how terrible the world was becoming. Apparently, there had been a big drug bust in the South Shore area, and the FBI was planning to make sure these guys went to jail for a very long time. As Lizzah passed by the television, she stopped to see what her parents were talking about. She recognized the building where the drug bust occurred as she had just left it about eight hours ago. She saw TJ, Eddie Ray and three of his other friends who were being taken out in handcuffs. Lizzah could not move nor speak. She just stood there in front of the TV motionless.

Finally, Lizzah got dressed and went to school. She could not function in the class, nor could she confide her frustrations in anyone. She sat in the lunchroom all day. She had to find Corrine to tell her what happened. She could help her through this. Corrine always had the answers. Lizzah knew Corrine would know what to do.

Chapter Nine
Living on the Edge

Corrine had a wonderful weekend. She could not wait to go to school to share her great news. Studying had not come easy for Corrine. She found herself with so many added responsibilities. For the last two years, she did laundry, cooked, and cleaned up the house. She made sure AJay and Cian, her two younger brothers, were clean and neat when they went to school. Now, at age seventeen, it was as if she had birthed these two children herself. At first, it was not so bad when her Mama was working. At least the rent was being paid, and there was money for food. Now, Mama hardly came home, and when she did, she just laid around the house. She was never sober enough to take care of any household business. Mama was not dependable now and had not made or contributed any money for over two years. This forced Corrine into a lifestyle she wanted no part of. Her mother did not know or care if the rent was paid. Until now, she had not told Big Mamma or her aunts what was happening. She knew If the authorities found out their mother was using heroin, all three of them would be split up and go into the foster care system. Corrine was not about to let that happen. At the age of fifteen, her neighbor secretly introduced her to a lucrative escort service. Corrine made friends quickly and, within six months, had over twenty wealthy repeat clients. She treated her clients well, and over time, most of them became her sponsors as opposed to clients. This made her well able to pay the bills. In short, Corrine was a high school student by day and a paid escort by night.

She was so angry with her mother. She hated her because her teenage life was almost gone now, and she had not enjoyed any of it. Watching her mother's destructive path made Corrine detest any type of drug, even an aspirin. She witnessed so many good people destroy their lives by using and selling. She didn't have a father because nobody ever told her who he was. The only people who were dependable lived over eight hundred miles away. If she stopped being an Escort, AJay and Cian would not survive, so Corrine had no choice.

Getting that scholarship was the answer to her prayers, and lately, she had been praying an awful lot. She had to get her degree, not only for herself but for her younger brothers. She would have to reach out to Big Mama and her Aunts Tiffany and Renee in Atlanta and finally let this secret out of the bag. Someone other than herself would have to take care of them for a while.

Corrine got to school too late to be admitted into her first class. She went to the lunchroom to study and get a little breakfast. She spotted Lizzah at a table all by herself and she was visibly upset. Corrine had been worried about her for a while because it was apparent to her that she was using something. She was so sweet and innocent when they met two years ago. She and Lizzah had instantly become good friends, but now, they barely talked to each other.

Corrine heard about Lizzah being with TJ. She knew that he loved her and seemed to protect her from everybody and everything. He showered her with gifts and took her everywhere. TJ had never shown that type of affection to anyone he dated, and he dated a lot of women.

Everyone always talked about TJ and how smart he was in school before he dropped out. Now, he heads the band and a business. He was successful in music and many other things. Her concern is that Lizzah is so young and so naive. Corrine did not think she was ready to handle TJ's lifestyle. She felt somewhat responsible for Lizzah ever since she met her at Freshman orientation. She was so talented, and her music was blowing up now, but she needed to stop drinking and smoking and focus on school and her career.

When Corrine joined her, Lizzah told her about her relationship with TJ and how much she loved him. She told her about the arrest and said she had left his condo a couple of hours before the raid. Lizzah told Corrine that she needed something to calm her nerves. TJ would always give her what was safe. She had no idea who to call or what to do. She could not talk to Robin or Henry because they would be very angry. If Henry found out she was dating a drug dealer and smoking, she would be put out of the house for sure. She did not know if she should find some of TJ's friends and try to get him out of jail or just let it play out and be there for him whenever he got out.

Lizzah was sobbing profusely now, and Corrine was concerned about her. "Well, my dear, you cannot come to my house because it is a big old ball of confusion there for sure," said Corrine. Lizzah laughed a little. They had another twenty-five minutes or so before the class period ended. They walked across the street to the park so they could finish talking in private.

Corrine told Lizzah a little about her situation at home and all about the scholarship she had just got to Texas A&M, and how it was all free. She was thrilled because she did not pay for housing, books, or food. Corrine would even get a stipend each month for transportation and personal items. All she had to do was maintain a 3.0 grade point average or better. Corrine told her she did not know how it happened, but it was official. Lizzah hugged her friend. She was so happy for her that she briefly forgot about TJ.

Corrine hugged her and they both cried. Finally, after a long embrace, Corrine said to Lizzah, "As for you, Missy, the best thing you can do now is to go home. The weekend is coming up, and you have not been performing for more than three weeks. I suggest you use this time to heal and sober up." She told Lizzah that she had not been smoking that long, so it would not be that difficult to quit. Corrine told Lizzah to focus on her music. "You need to get ready to find a new band. The Feds have gotten involved with TJ's case, and they want to make an example out of him and his friends!" She told her that she believes TJ, Eddie Ray, and (The Band) will do some real-time. This news made Lizzah start crying all over again. Later that day, Lizzah tried to visit TJ in the County Jail but was denied entrance. Finally, she took Corrine's advice and went home.

For the next two days, all Lizzah wanted to do was sleep and cry. She knew she would not be able to sleep for long because nobody stayed in bed in Robin's house after 9:30 am. She was surprised when Robin knocked on her bedroom door at about 11:00 that morning and invited her to see a musical. They laughed and talked with each other for about three hours. Lizzah told her a little about her relationship with TJ.

Robin hugged Lizzah and told her how much she loved her. Robin reminded Lizzah that she was her child and that she would love her no matter what. Because Lizzah was always either rebellious or just gone, they had not enjoyed each other's company like this since their time in California. Although she was still sad about TJ, Lizzah accepted the invitation and had a good time with her mother.

She looked forward to spending more time with Robin and even Henry. Lizzah knew that Henry was not happy with her. He told her it was because she grew up. Lizzah thought her dad was just weird. During the next few weeks, Lizzah went to school every day. She went to every class on time and, for the most part, was beginning to enjoy it. She could hear the whispers about her and what had happened to TJ. She noticed the strange looks of some of the other students and even some teachers. She somehow found the strength to keep going without falling apart. She missed TJ so much, but she knew Corrine was right. She had to focus on finding another musician for her upcoming performances. Lizzah promised herself she would start taking school more seriously and had some hard work to do.

Six groups had offered to work with Lizzah. She managed to narrow it down to just two. Skip's group, The True-Blue Boys, sounded good. Johnny had worked with them several times when he needed backup help for his concerts.

There was a new group that had just formed but they could not agree on a name. Currently, they call themselves "The Group". Lizzah thought they were good. She decided to rehearse with them and, she was feeling good about the results. Two weeks later, Lizzah and The Group sang "Only Your Love" at a concert.

A week after the show, the song was blowing all over WCVI radio in Chicago. Later, they learned It was on radio stations in Detroit, Philadelphia, and Atlanta. Lizzah was once again extremely busy with school and performances every weekend. She missed TJ terribly and decided the song would be a tribute to him and their love for each other. There was no time to be sad or idle any more, and she wished him all the best. She had nothing but warm thoughts of TJ, and she would always cherish the love they had. She vowed to continue writing to him every week, even if he never wrote back to her.

Chapter Ten
Golden Opportunity

As a Junior in high school, Lizzah had a lot of decisions to make. She and The Group were to perform at local spots every weekend for the next four months. They were encouraged by Jam Radio to audition for the next big Jamestown tour. Should they win, it would be a great opportunity, an excellent jumpstart for their career. The only problem was it would take Lizzah away from school and she would have to use the Jamestown tutors to complete her classwork. Lizzah knew that neither Robin nor Henry would allow her to leave Chicago for a tour because her grades were low. The good thing was that even If they did not get selected to go on tour, The Group was still busy until the end of the year. Lizzah wanted and needed to rest, but she did not know how.

She and The Group got along well. She was their little sister, and they were her brothers. Lizzah loved being the only girl in the bunch and they all complimented each other.

There were the two identical twins, Lonnie and Ronnie. Ronnie played a mean sax, and Lonnie played bass guitar. Both were good, but Ronnie and Lonnie were tricksters. Because they were identical, few people could tell them apart. Their personalities told a story of their own. Lonnie was wild and outgoing, and Ronnie was quite laid back. When they wanted to, they could mimic each other's personalities and confuse everyone, but they couldn't mimic each other's talents. Most people could not tell them apart until they started playing music.

Then there was Ralph (Preacher Boy) Leftridge on lead guitar. He was the most mellow one of the entire group and the peacemaker of everyone. His parents were both ministers in the Baptist church. Ralph's family alienated him when he started playing secular music. He had to move into a shelter to complete his education and play his music. He was always praying and singing hymns.

Sabastian was on the keyboard. He was an extremely talented concert pianist. Sabastian often told everyone how his grandmother made him spend countless hours practicing and playing for recitals before she died. He said she was merciless. He had to play for the church choir every Sunday and rehearsals every Friday. Three other days after school, he had to practice various pieces of music for two hours each night after he finished his homework. Sebastian's grandmother's dream was for him to become a world-renowned concert pianist. Because of his musical exposure, he could play all types of music. The only problem was that Sebastian only loved the blues, and he loved the Jamestown Sound. What made Sebastian so unique to the group was that he knew how to mix the music together, even if just a split second, and achieve amazing results. His music style mesmerized the crowd at every performance as they never knew what to expect. Lizzah thought Sebastian was adorable. Her attraction to him frightened her a bit, mostly because of her past relationship with TJ. Sebastian was at least twelve years older than she, and Lizzah thought it best to keep their relationship professional.

Finally, Johnny, Lizzah's former singing partner, joined the group. Lizzah knew they would all make beautiful music together.

To be considered for Jamestown, The Group was required to have a stage name. Everyone was satisfied with just being known as "The Group," but that was not acceptable to Jamestown. The promotors told them that if they did not present themselves with a name, Jamestown would choose one for them. None of them wanted that to happen. Lizzah had fond memories of her childhood and her Uncle's big black motorcycle. As a small child, she would pick at the bike emblem. She was fascinated with the big gold wings that she tried for about five years to take off the bike. Each year, her Uncle told her the same thing.

Baby, why do you want Unca B's Goldwing? He told her that the cycle would not be the same and the wing needed to stay on the bike. He would buy her a bunch of doll toys and even get her a Slinky one time. Her Unca B was not parting with that emblem, though. It was a beautiful little wing made of pure gold. To Lizzah, the little gold wing symbolizes success and freedom. She believed their music would spread happiness to everyone who heard it, and their success would come swiftly like on wings of gold. Thus, they decided to name "The Group" "The Goldwings."

"The Goldwings" all got along really well. They were very close, and they were each other's family. They were all beginning to be concerned about Ralph and Sebastian. The were beginning to be concerned about Sebastian. He was good at what he did but was always high. The truth was that mostly all the were dependent on either marijuana or alcohol to function. Lizzah was no exception. She continued to go to most of her classes and finish her coursework. It was important to Robin and TJ that she finish high school and that is what she intended to do no matter how she felt inside. She thought of TJ a lot. On several occasions, she had tried to visit him, but he was always either in solitary confinement or had refused her visit. She prayed every day that one of their songs would go platinum and they would be well on their way. There would be no need for college. She was proud of her friend Corrine but held to her belief that college was not for everyone, and it certainly was not for her.

Months had passed, and finally, they got the good news. The Goldwings had been chosen to participate in the Jamestown concert. After much pleading and crying, Lizzah was finally able to convince Robin and Henry to let her go. Jamestown would select two of the four groups to be perfected and groomed to Jamestown standards. These groups would not only get a contract but would also get salary-paid tours to New York City, Atlanta, Chicago, Pennsylvania, and Los Angeles. The winners would be an overnight success. Everyone was happy for her, but Robin was concerned about Lizzah completing school. Lizzah assured her mother that she would finish, but deep in her heart, she did not want to return at all. When she arrived at Jamestown, Lizzah was not prepared for the cut-throat competition and the animosity between some of the groups. She did welcome the vocal challenges and was learning and enjoying everything she could. The male groups were nice to her, and, for the most part, she got along with everyone. Bill Brady's group was called The Hearts of Gold. They were a smooth crooning group from Pennsylvania. They were some hard-working, nice guys, and everyone loved their harmonic sound. They also had some unique dance moves and were always in perfect rhythm with each other. They won, hands down, by the judges in all of their performances.

The Soundbytes were another male group from Jacksonville, Florida. They were good, but they were antisocial. They did not agree amongst themselves at first and fought about everything. People would never believe how much they argued if you saw them on stage. Darryl, the lead singer, was always in Lizzah's face, talking about how they were better than everyone else and that he knew his group was going to be one of the finals to go to the tour. He was trying to convince Lizzah to dump the Goldwings and sing with his group. Lizzah told him that she and the Goldwings were a family. She said the Goldwings moved together, or they did not move at all. Lizzah liked Darryl as a person, though. She knew that he was having fun. It didn't take long for him and all of the Goldwings to become best friends.

Another group was Carmelita and the Georgettes from Atlanta, Georgia. They were nice people. This group was okay, but Lizzah did not think they could sing very well. She doubted they could make the finals, but she wished them well.

There was another girl group, the Eight-Faces of Eve, which was talented and had a tight sound. They danced semi slutty and made a lot of forbidden moves. Gigi was the lead singer of the group, and she was nobody's punk. The best way to describe Gigi would be like a ball of confusion. Gigi raised a lot of hell with Lonnie, our Sax player. She hated Lizzah, Carmelita and anybody that she felt was a good competitor.

Gigi was so combative that for a minute, even Lizzah thought about giving up and going home. Everyone joked about Gigi, saying she was at least five of the eight faces all by herself. Nobody knew what to expect of her from one moment to the next. Darryl said that Gigi was just mad because Lonnie would not sleep with her like he had, along with all of the Soundbytes. Lonnie told Lizzah that Gigi could perform well and was pretty, but thanks but no thanks. Everybody would laugh and laugh. Ms. Lottie was the Fashion manager for all the groups signed at Jamestown. Ms. Lottie dressed all the groups. She created a unique Image for every entertainer. She did not play with anyone, nor did she compromise. Many of the performers hated Ms. Lottie and had real problems with the wardrobes she chose for them. The men had problems with the pink, red, and loud colored suits and glittering shoes Ms. Lottie designed for them.

Darryl told her that men did not wear pink and that he refused to wear it. The women had all kinds of complaints about the clothes being too tight, too big, or the material itched. Some wanted to wear too much makeup, and others did not want to wear makeup at all. Everyone hated those long hot wigs. Everything got ugly when the stylists started cutting hair and changing hair colors.

Lizzah herself was distraught with her new hairstyle, saying it looked like a dismantled spaceship. Nobody understood where Ms. Lottie was going with these appearances. Gigi's complaint got to Stephen James, and he was very upset about it. He stood by his auntie, Ms. Lottie. Mr. James called a meeting with everyone. He insisted they follow all house and wardrobe rules or go home. He said he did not care if any of them went home, and there were plenty of people waiting in line for the opportunity that he had given them. Darryl politely wore the pink suit and the rime stone shoes.

Gigi grudgingly submitted to the hairdresser and makeup artists, but her attitude was still bad. Nothing was said about the wardrobe, rehearsal times, or any other issues and nobody got sent home.

A few weeks went by, and Lizzah could not get enough sleep. There just were not enough hours in a single day to finish everything, she thought to herself. They went out to a party for a few hours on the first weekend she came to Jamestown. The next month after her arrival, her days consisted of early morning coursework, vocal exercises, speech therapy, image sharpening, and extensive rehearsals six days a week.

On Sundays, everyone slept. A few went to church or to parties, but there were no rehearsals. By the time Sunday rolled around, everyone was exhausted. Most Sundays, Lizzah did not get up until 3:00 in the afternoon. She spent that time talking with Robin and Henry on the telephone, assuring them she was behaving herself. She spoke with Corrine, who was now away in college. Often, they talked about everything from college, TJ's trial, the competition, and even Corrine's little brothers and how well they were adjusting in their new home in Georgia.

She said her Aunt Rene had full custody of them and they were doing well in school. Lizzah talked so long on the phone the Jamestown administrators threatened to take away her phone privileges and make her pay a portion of the phone bill. The next Sunday, Lizzah, Carmelita, and a few of the Soundbytes decided they would go out and have a little fun. Everyone wanted to check out the new movie, "Superfly." Most of them were out of it, but nobody fell asleep because the film was really good. After the movie, they stopped by Bakers Lounge on Livernois Ave. Baker's was a nice place with a perfect vibe. There was one couple in there that was not having such a good time. They were fighting and arguing about everything from wanting ice in their water to the serving size of the French fries. The man accused the girl of being unfaithful, and the girl denied everything. For the most part, the girl was quiet, but the man never shut up. It did not take long to see that the man was very intoxicated. Although the couple was causing a huge scene, they decided to stay there to eat. They ordered pizza, chicken wings, Hopingators and a lot of beer.

They were sitting there a long while, just laughing and having a good time. Finally, the couple that was arguing left, and they enjoyed themselves even more. To their surprise, Bakers offered live entertainment on Sunday evenings when most clubs and businesses closed early to honor the Sabbath day. They stayed a couple of hours longer. They promised one another that they would do more fun things together on Sundays when they were free.

As they walked to Darryl's car, they prayed it would start. They were mostly from other cities, and they were not familiar with this area of Detroit. Both Lizzah and Carmelita had commented earlier that they should not tarry in the neighborhood. As they continued walking, Lizzah heard a faint moaning sound as she passed by an old, dried shrub on their way to the car. It was almost midnight, and there were no street or even porch lights on. They walked a few more feet, and this time they heard a loud cry. Carmelita ran toward the sound to investigate, and everyone else followed her. Once again, they heard the whimper and then a loud cry saying, "Please, help me." Darryl said he thought it was a setup, and he turned to leave immediately. He said he didn't want to be involved in any trouble. Carmelita took out a pocket flashlight and she and Lizzah continued to look.

It was Lizzah who spotted the small, frail figure lying on the ground. She could see a trickle of blood on her lip, and her clothes were badly torn. The lady said that her ankle hurt badly. Said she and her boyfriend were in the restaurant earlier. Her boyfriend was drunk and had thrown her out of his car and refused to take her home. Darryl offered to call an ambulance, but the girl said that her father would find out if she called the police. She said if her father knew, there would be hell to pay. She asked Darryl if he would please just take her home. Reluctantly, Darryl agreed and they all helped her get into the car. It wasn't until they were in front of her home that Lizzah recognized her. The girl they brought home was Stephen James's daughter, Ada Grace.

CHAPTER ELEVEN
LIES AND DECEPTION

Lizzah was still excited about the fun time they all had on Sunday. She had not been able to relax in a long time. Between the tutoring sessions, coursework, and the constant rehearsals, there was little time to do anything except study, practice, and more practice. Lizzah was learning new songs every day. Before the competition, she had never been a fan of jazz or the blues. Stephen James, now affectionately known as Pappa J wanted to expand her knowledge beyond soul music. He directed his Staff Assistant, Mr. Ray, to have her rehearse some jazz and blues material. Mr. Ray wanted to record some of his new soundtracks. If they could prove themselves in the competition, he would use the Goldwings to record the material. The first song Mr. Ray introduced to her was, The Blues Has Taken Over by Betty Davis. Lizzah had difficulty getting into the pieces, and to her, they were just dull. She did welcome the challenge of learning the new material. Of course, Sebastian had no problem working on the material, as that was his specialty. His experience and Lizzah's voice appealed to Mr. Ray, and he was looking forward to recording his music with them. Unlike most competitions, these groups were very close, and everyone was like a family. They shared opinions and ideas, and they encouraged each other. The only exception was Gigi. Nobody knew which face Gigi was going to reveal that day. Gigi hated every directive she was given. If it was not her idea, she hated it, and in her mind, she was always right. Gigi and The Eight Faces fought about everything. She did not get along with any of the other groups and was extremely jealous of Lizzah. After a very short while, everyone knew if there was any confusion at all, Gigi either knew about it or was directly responsible.

Her disdain for Lizzah grew more intense because of the special assignment given to her. Gigi did everything she could to discredit Lizzah. She even demanded that Mr. Ray let her audition to sing a blues piece with Sebastian without Lizzah. She spreads lies about Lizzah, telling everyone she knows that she and Mr. Ray were in a relationship, and that was why she was getting special treatment. This lie made it back to Pappa J. and he became very angry with Gigi. He suspended Gigi from the rehearsals for one week. Gigi's performances were good despite the confusion that she always caused. Staff was told to give her another chance and that they had to work with her. She pretended to like Carmelita but spoke badly about her to all the other competitors. Nobody could understand why Gigi was so hateful because she was talented. She and The Eight Faces sounded good. They had a great chance of winning the competition if Gigi would get her attitude together.

For the next week, Mr. Ray would swap the lead singers. Gigi worked on the blues material with the Goldwings and Lizzah substituted as the lead for Eight Faces of Eve. Lizzah felt so heartbroken and out of place.

Although she performed well with the Eight Faces, it was hard for her to process what was going on. Gigi did not do so well with the Goldwings though, and they had Sebastian to thank for that. None of them knew that this was the beginning of a setup from Jamestown officials to get Gigi eliminated from the program.

Lizzah was glad to see Sunday come so she could once again relax. Although she was able to sound good with the Eight Faces, she was in a bad headspace because of Gigi. She and the Goldwings were a family, she thought to herself. She had a completely different genre and vibe than Gigi. She was finding it very hard to stay positive and productive. Rather than go out with the others, she chose to just stay home and rest.

Despite smoking three special cigarettes, her heart was hurting. She could not understand how Gigi could cause so much confusion. She was afraid that all the rehearsing she and Sebastian had done was for nothing. Lizzah did not know how to go on with the competition and even worse, no longer wanted to. She didn't understand why the music professionals did not see what was happening. For hours, she just sat silently crying and staring into space.

Sebastian was worried about Lizzah. He had never ever seen his little stage wife in this frame of mind. He had to do something because they had come too far not to finish the course. Every Sunday, Lizzah would be hogging the payphone talking to her family and her friends. That day, she did nothing but cry and cry some more. Everyone was planning to meet at the new nightspot for drinks and a barbecue. While Lizzah slept, Lonnie, Sebastian, Carmelita, two of the Georgettes, and The Hearts all met at The Haughty Pig on Six Mile Road. The conversation of the evening was obviously "what to do about Gigi?" They had to develop a plan. The plan had to work, they thought, and it had to work quickly.

Chapter Twelve
ROAD TO RECOVERY

It had been only two weeks since Ada Grace was released from the rehabilitation center. Since returning to her home, she stayed away from everyone, including Aunt Lottie and her father. Now Ada Grace had the daunting task of convincing him of her sobriety, enough to resume her position. She still remembered that embarrassing incident last month when Cedric had hurt her so badly and left her bleeding near someone's driveway. That would never happen again, she thought to herself. She simply had to pull herself together, and she had to do it quickly. Ada Grace knew she was healing now because she had gained most of her weight back, and she was always hungry. She and Cedric had not spoken since that night, and she hoped to never lay eyes on him again. Ada Grace had to convince her father to let her have her job back. She decided to go to The Haughty Pig to taste this barbecue and shrimp platter everyone was talking about. She was looking forward to drinking a few apple margaritas but thought maybe that wasn't a good idea. She had not planned to be out long because she had an early morning meeting at Jamestown.

She knew it would be a challenge because her father would want an explanation of everything. She would have to hear how she repeatedly made such bad choices and, now, what narcotics she was taking and when she started taking them. He would then tell her how many sacrifices he had made for her since she came to live with him so she wouldn't end up like her mother. Blah, blah, blah. He was delusional, she thought. She wished she could tell him how she really felt about him.

For a long time, she hadn't known who her father was. As a child, she didn't understand why he never came to celebrate birthdays or graduations. She knew that she could never be prepared for this meeting with him, but she had to do something. Dad had been quiet, but she knew he would make her do something, and she did not want to go back to school.

So far, she was impressed with the atmosphere in The Haughty Pig. This place had a game room, bowling alley, billiards, and a rooftop deck. If the food was good, she would certainly make it her weekly hangout.

She saw a large group that was laughing loudly and having a good time. She recognized one man, though. She believed he was one of the people who drove her home last month. She and Cedric had argued at Bakers that night and she was intoxicated. The last thing she remembered was being thrown out of his car. Ada Grace was too drunk to walk, and her ankle hurt badly. Despite every effort she made that night, she could not move. She did not see the other girl that was with them that night. After listening to them talk for a while, she knew they were the Jamestown talent contestants. It was clear they had gotten to know her sister/ cousin Gigi and that she had vexed them all. They wanted revenge on her badly. This could be her chance, she thought. She wished the other girl was there so she would have an excuse to interrupt, introduce herself, and thank her. She decided to use the incident as an excuse to intrude on their conversation. She had to get the man's attention, and she had to do it before it was too late.

Darry took the invitation from the bartender's hand. He politely accepted the woman's invitation to join her at the table. At first glance, Darryl could tell this woman was not his type. She was impeccably dressed, especially for being in a neighborhood barbeque joint on a Sunday night. Everything about her screamed high maintenance yet, there was another vibe he got from her warning him she could be extremely damaged goods. She looked vaguely familiar to him, but he could not place where their paths had crossed. Nevertheless, Darryl always welcomed a good conversation.

"You look lovely," Darryl said as he approached her table. "Thank you," she replied as she dropped her head. Surprised by this new shift in her demeanor, Darryl extended his hand. "I'm Darryl. What is your name?" "I'm Ada; they call me Ada Grace." "Lovely name," Darryl replied. "A sweet name for a beautiful lady." "Thank you," Ada said as she dropped her head once again.

"Listen, I didn't mean to pull you away from your friends. I believe you and your friends were at Bakers Cafe a little over a month ago. My boyfriend and I got into a huge fight. It's not something that has ever happened to me before. You and your friends took me home that night. I just wanted to say thank you."

Darryl looked at her in shock. He remembered that night very well. He would never have guessed that this beautiful woman seated in front of him was the same frail person they had taken home just over a month ago.

They talked for a while. He told her he grew up in Jacksonville, Florida, and had left everything behind to compete. He and his group, The Soundbytes, were all homeless before Jamestown accepted them. Now we live day-to-day, he explained. Ada shared a little information about her family and her relationship with Cedric. She vowed never to talk to him again. She mentioned that she had overheard them talking about the music and asked if all of them were Jamestown contestants. Darryl confirmed that they all were, and they came from various groups and cities. He began to tell her about Gigi and her group, the Eight Faces of Eve. He said the competitions were becoming a nightmare, and it was only one person who was continuously keeping the confusion going. Ada smiled and then laid the second bombshell on Darryl. She explained to him that she was Ada Grace James and that Stephen James was her father. She told him that Gigi was her cousin. Gigi's mother, Aunt Fayrene, was her father's baby sister, and they have never got along with each other. She said Gigi is cutting up because she believes she is a guaranteed winner because she is family. Gigi does not think my father will eliminate her, but nothing could be further from the truth. Darryl motioned to the waitress to add one more seat at the group table upon hearing this news. He insisted that Ada Grace share this news with the rest of the group.

Everyone was skeptical at first, but Ada Grace assured them that Jamestown was already setting Gigi up to go home. She assured everyone it was a done deal and that Gigi would not be a problem for long. Sebastian introduced himself to Ada and told her about Lizzah and how distraught she was about Gigi. He told her they had left Lizzah at home, crying her eyes out. Sabastian told Ada Grace that Lizzah was the one who had insisted they help her on the night of the incident. At that moment, it all came back to her. She remembered Lizzah very well now. She saw her perform in Chicago a few times. Lizzah had not come to her for help with her group, but she saw her perform quite often. She always thought Lizzah had a beautiful voice, but she was very young and kind of naive. She also remembered that Lizzah was TJ's girlfriend before he got in trouble with the Feds. Now she finds that this young girl was someone who had gone out of her way to make sure she was safe. She assured everyone that Gigi's reign of terror would be ending very soon. Ada Grace wanted to talk to Lizzah but would not do it at Jamestown. They would have to meet tomorrow, and Lizzah would have to follow the plan.

Darryl and Sebastian could hardly wait to tell Lizzah about meeting Ada Grace. They told her the new information they had learned, and immediately, the sadness went away. Lizzah was initially puzzled as to why Ada Grace wasn't involved in the competition. She was even more surprised to see her in a domestic situation but kept quiet about it.

The next day, after the rehearsals were over, Lizzah, Sebastian and Ada Grace met at the Haughty Pig. Ada Grace assured Lizzah and Sebastian that the promoters put Gigi with Mr. Ray as a setup. He knows that Gigi won't be able to adapt to that style. Gigi performs well in what she knows, but she will not handle what Mr. Ray will give her. Ada Grace assured them that everyone was sick of Gigi's mess. Still, her Dad does not want to deal with his baby sister. My Dad will eliminate her if she makes him look bad, and that is what they are planning to do. Ada Grace said the best thing Lizzah can do is to be herself. Don't try to get revenge and stop arguing with her. Your job now is to rock your performances with the Eight Faces.

Everyone has seen your sweet and wholesome side. Let everyone know how talented you are by decently adapting to her semi-raunchy style. Ada Grace told them the good news: she was back working with Jamestown. Her assignment was to help Lizzah work on the number with the Eight Faces. You got this girl, trust me., Ada Grace assured Lizzah. Lizzah regained hope in the success of her performance. She was now looking forward to working with Ada Grace and watching all the drama unfold.

Chapter Thirteen
The Plan

Ray was up bright and early, pacing the floor and thinking. He could not sleep because the music for his assigned number was not quite right. He was more than agitated by how Stephen James was running things lately. What was he doing, Ray wondered, and what the hell was a "Pappa J" anyway? There is a dark, unsettling presence surrounding this child, and Ray more than hates working with her. Because she was Jamestown's family, he had to waste his precious time working with this little boisterous, troublemaking teenager. The girl was bad news, and beyond the gyrating and tick-tocking, he thought, she possessed no real talent. Gigi would be gone in a matter of days, and he would see to that. There was no way he would ever use her to record any of his music. He had warned Stephen James at the beginning that this girl could do little more than shimmy and shake, but no, he had to give "his precious niece" a chance. With the company's reputation at stake, this was no time for him to be getting soft.

Ray heard how upset Lizzah was about singing with The Eight Faces, but he could not tell her their plans. Lizzah was strong, he thought, and she was very talented.

She even added a twist of style to the slutty material she worked on with the Eight Faces. Ray was glad to hear that Ada Grace was back. She could help Lizzah perfect the sound he was looking for. He doubted the Eight Faces would last long enough for Lizzah to sing even one number with them. He was right. Mr. Ray and Sebastian were just about to go over the new material when he heard the news of Gigi's arrest. He was relieved to hear that he no longer needed to execute his plans. Gigi had finally eliminated her own group from the competition.

Everyone knew Gigi always started trouble, so nobody but the Eight Faces listened to anything she said. Everyone thought she was just mentally unstable and craved a lot of attention. Gigi was doing many underhanded things. When plans didn't go her way, she became angry and combative. The last straw was two days ago when Gigi went to the police station and filed a police report on poor Bill Brady. She said he had beaten her and tried to rape her. Pappa J found out about it because the police were now involved, and the situation had to be dealt with. Bill was taken to the police station and questioned for six long hours. Poor Bill was crying and pleading with the police. Bill told them that he really had no clue what was going on because he and Gigi barely spoke to each other. The Sergeant believed Bill from the very beginning. He had an undercover officer dressed as a civilian under arrest and placed the officer and Gigi together in a secluded waiting room. The Sergeant apologized profusely for the long wait and bought them pizza, burgers and soda. As they devoured the food, Gigi began talking to her newfound friend. Gigi not knowing her new friend's status, admitted she had made the whole thing up. She even told her how she went into the alley and beat herself in the face with two big rocks. She said she wanted the Hearts to be eliminated because she was afraid his group would be picked over her group. Bill Brady was released immediately, and Papa J came personally to bring him back to Jamestown. Gigi was arrested Immediately was charged with filing a false police report.

When everyone found out what Gigi had done, they were very angry. Surely, after this stunt, Papa J would eliminate Gigi from the contest, and they were right. With Papa J's assistance, Bill filed charges against Gigi and got a restraining order against her immediately. When released from jail, Papa J personally eliminated Gigi. She and the Eight Faces were told to leave Jamestown property immediately. While the other Seven Faces were sorrowful, Gigi went temporarily insane. She went from hurling death threats to crying profusely. Somebody said they overheard her tell Papa J she was going to tell her mother about him. While it was entertaining to some, others looked at her with pity. Finally, they thought, the contest would now go on, and they would have fun in a drama-free environment.

The next few weeks flew by, and for the first time in weeks, there were no arguments and no drama. Ada Grace was working well with everyone, and they were glad to see her. There were only two weeks before showtime, and in the end, only two of the four groups would go on tour. They studied. They worked hard and, most importantly, loved the music they were making. A few of them thought they saw Gigi and a few of The Faces hanging around outside but didn't pay them any attention. Those weeks flew by, and nobody mentioned Gigi nor the Faces at all.

Chapter Fourteen
SHOWTIME

The reality was setting in for the contestants as the show would begin in just one day. The fliers promoting the concert were out in all the neighborhoods. There were commercials on all the local channels advertising the two-night Blue Carpet event. Ada Grace was busy tweaking the last-minute vocal changes. There were four dress rehearsals, and Lizzah had to face the fact that none of her outfits would be comfortable. The dress Ms. Lottie made for her opening number itched and stuck every inch of her body. To make things worse, she had enough fake hair on top of her head that she was sure a few creatures could comfortably live in there. It felt like her head weighed over a ton. She decided to take a few pulls off her special cigarette to help her feel more comfortable. Next, she was on to dress rehearsal for her makeup. When she saw the thick brown paste and two-inch long eyelashes, she wondered what creature she would look like during this show. She had no idea how bizarre she would look at show-time. She did know that she had to deliver a performance of a lifetime.

Cobo Hall was at full capacity, and people were standing all in the front aisles. Speakers were put outside of the Hall so that passers-by could hear the show, and local news stations were everywhere. Word had spread that the Malone family and a few other well-known artists would stop by. Lizzah was very nervous. She realized that tonight's show will be seen worldwide, and the fear nearly crippled her. What if her voice failed, she thought to herself, or her timing was off. She was relieved when Sebastian handed her a small pill to help her calm down even more. She also took two more drags of her special cigarette and shared some of it with Sebastian. That is enough, she thought as she drifted into an unexplained calmness.

The four judges were there and they were a sight for sore eyes. What was odd about these judges was that nobody, that was anybody, knew who they were. Later in the show, they learned that none of them had any musical background. These people were chosen solely due to the size of the donation they gave to the Jamestown Corporation. Lizzah pondered this new information. She had to stay focused and give her best performance tonight, she thought to herself. Their job was to rate each performance between one and five. A rating of one meant the lowest performance and five meant the performance was outstanding.

Carmelita and the Georgettes were the first act to go on stage. The Georgettes opened the show with a slow melody of "Yes I'm Ready" by Barbara Mason. They looked amazingly beautiful as their dresses shimmered with silvery glitter. Ms. Lottie had designed glittery high-heeled shoes for them that matched their dresses. They sounded lovely, but due to several wardrobe malfunctions, they were afraid to move around. They sang so beautifully that nobody in the audience noticed their anxiety about the wardrobe. Ada Grace stood behind the stage proudly as their angelic sound drew thunderous applause from the audience. The judges did not look impressed at all. These judges were a strange bunch, Lizzah thought to herself. They did not smile, clap, or sway, nor did they offer feedback. They just studied each group and wrote on notepads.

Next to the stage were the Soundbytes. These men wore light blue polyester suits and white silk shirts. They all sported light blue and white shoes and blue ties, and each of them wore silver pocket hankies with a silver pocket watch. The hairdresser had processed their hair so tight that no amount of water could make it frizz or move. They opened with a song by The Drifters, Stand by Me, and finished with one of James Brown's new songs, Get Up off of That Thang. Their harmony was majestic. They were in step, and Darryl even mimicked the King's famous Moonwalk. People were all in the Isles dancing. A few people tried to bum-rush the stage, and Jamestown security had to escort a few people out of the Hall. Nobody knew that Robert Harris was going to be the Master of Ceremony. People were shocked when he came on stage. The crowd came together quickly when the first word out of his mouth was, "Y'all sit cho asses down. Sit down ya here. Now don't nobody belong on dis here damn stage but the people up hea sangin. If ya ain't sangin sit cho ass down. Y'all act like dem kids dat be running round da neighborhood. Dem some badass kids. Sit cho asses down. Don't brang dat in hea." At that moment, everybody laughed, but they made their way back to their seats. He even had the judges snickering as he talked about his neighbor's badass kids. To Lizzah, this was the first sign that those judges were enjoying anything.

During intermission, Lizzah peaked out from the curtain and saw Robin, Henry, and Corrine. She could not visit with them yet because she had not performed. She knew they all said they would try to make opening night a few weeks ago, but she had not spoken with them since. She was delighted to see them. Robin and Henry were impeccably dressed, as always. Carmelita had play-flirted with Henry throughout her performance. Backstage, she plots to steal Henry from his wife. Carmelita told everyone backstage that Robin had just looked at her like she smelled of bad fish when she started flirting with Henry. That plot ceased quickly when Carmelita found out it was Lizzah's father she had flirted with onstage. Everyone laughed and was having a great time. Corrine had come from Texas to see Lizzah perform. She was so happy to see her, and they had a lot of catching up to do.

Lizzah was glad to see the Malone Family. Backstage, Reggie congratulated her for working hard enough even to be a contestant. The Malone's, along with Liz and Conchita performed their brand-new single "What Chu Gonna Do," and the crowd was dancing once again. Following the family's performance, Reggie sang his first hit single, Lonely in the Dark, and Women started fainting. As he left the stage, a woman took off her panties and threw them on the stage.

The undies almost hit Robert Williams in the face as he was coming on stage, and he frantically fanned them away. "Unn you nasty," Robert shouted as he dodged the undergarments and went onto the stage. "Look, don't chall tho dem nasty thangs up hea. Keep all yo under clothes on yall here me. Gon hurt somebody wit dat." Fanning his nose he said, "Where yall thank y'all at a Micha Jackson concert!" The crowd went crazy with laughter. Somebody get dem thangs outa here and gimme da Lysol spray. Immediately someone came from backstage with a big oversized can of Lysol spray, and the crowd again went crazy with laughter.

The Goldwings were the next to the stage. Each of the fellas was decked out in Kelly Green suits, glittering gold shirts with green and gold hats. Lonnie did not hide the fact that he was not happy about the way he looked. Lizzah had on a shimmering black dress that scooped up on one side of her leg. The back of the dress was so low cut that it stopped a little before her buttocks began. She wore a see-through Kelly green coat that split up the sides. The coat had a small train that flowed as Lizzah walked across the stage. The material itched and stuck. She had on three-inch glass slippers, but she did not feel like Cinderella. Her hair was so heavy on her head that she had to practice moving her head around in the mirror so she would not appear awkward.

Ada Grace picked two songs for Lizzah. The first was "Take Me" by Mable John, and the second was "Fever" by Peggy Lee. Lizzah thought the first song, Take Me, was depressing and boring, but Sebastian had an idea. They put their heads together and found a fantastic way to combine a bunch of songs. Lizzah came on stage, making small, graceful steps and singing Barbara Mason's hit single. The coat moved along the sides of her legs, exposing a little thigh but not much. The judges did not seem impressed so far. In the second stanza of the song, Lizzah walks over to Sebastian, rubs his cheek, then brings her thumb downward and rests it on his lips. Sebastian stops in his tracks as if Mesmerized by her touch. He and Lonnie would abruptly break out into a classic duo of Full Moon and Empty Arms on the piano. The crowd stared in surprise as if waiting to see exactly where they were going with this number.

After just one stanza, Lizzah takes three steps backward, shimmying to the beat of the drum. The coat falls to the floor, and Lizzah dances and sings Fever. The crowd standing goes wild. One of the judges is now standing up, and another has his tongue hanging out of his mouth. Lizzah saw her parents smiling, and Robin was crying. Corrine stared in utter disbelief. Once backstage, Ada Grace grabbed Lizzah and hugged her. That was amazing. You are going to win this thing, girl. Just wait until they see your performance tomorrow night.

The Hearts of Gold were next to the stage, dressed in Pale Pink suits, shimmering silver shoes, and shirts. They had on pale pink derby hats, and each of them sported a straight silver cane. Bill Brady was not too happy with the outfits at first. That all changed when the curtain opened, and they all began to sing. The Hearts of Gold started with one of the Stylistic's songs, Stone in Love with You. Their voices were sensational, and they were in step. Their last performance was one of The Temptations' new songs, "Get Ready Cause Here I Come."

At the end of the show, The Malone Family performed another of their hit singles, Something About Your Smile. All of the groups returned to the stage for the final song of the night: Reach Out and Touch Somebody's Hand by The Supremes. The first night of the show was ended.

Everyone would have to wait until tomorrow to find out who would be moving forward to night two. The thought of winning and touring was becoming a reality to Lizzah, and it was overwhelming. Her dreams were about to come true, she thought to herself. So much has happened for her today, she thought, and the night is still young. She changed her clothes and quickly ran out to meet her parents and best friend. Lizzah was exhausted, happy, and tired, but she could not stop moving.

CHAPTER FIFTEEN
I SEE YOU

It had been over two months since Lizzah had seen her parents. She missed them so much. She hugged Robin and cried when she hugged Henry. She invited them, along with Corrine, to her dressing room to hang out. They told her they would only see tonight's show because Henry had to be back at work tomorrow night. Lizzah brought her parents up to speed about everything. How competitive the groups had been at first and the whole Gigi ordeal. They all told her how great she was tonight, and Henry had to admit that he had not expected her to perform as well as she did. They got a real kick out of her outfit, and they all thought her hair was amazing. Lizzah told them all the stories about costume, hair, and makeup fiascos, and all of them laughed and had a great time. Henry told Lizzah that Jamestown needed to keep Ms. Lottie because everybody's outfits were fantastic. Lizzah jokingly told Henry she was going to buy him a pink and silver suit for Christmas. The thought of Henry in such a get-up made Robin laugh. Henry said he didn't need any pink or silver suit because he wasn't performing anywhere. Robin said she was excited and impressed, and because of Lizzah, they may end up moving back to California after all.

Corrine said she was also surprised at how everyone performed and that the Goldwings should win hands down. Corrine told Lizzah she didn't have to fly out until Monday. She would be at the Saturday show. She left Lizzah and her parents and went straight to her hotel room. Lizzah introduced Robin and Henry to the rest of the Goldwings, and they all talked for hours. At around two in the morning, Lizzah walked with her parents to their car. They told her they would stay the night at the Best Western on Eight Mile Road and check out the next morning.

A pair of blinding bright headlights appeared out of nowhere and they were coming straight toward them. Terrified, Lizzah froze in her tracks. Robin quickly moved from the street, pulling Lizzah with her. Then, there was total darkness. The car had cut the lights and stopped about 20 feet away from them. The women in the car laughed loudly. She heard one of them say take that and continued laughing. Next time I won't miss you. As the car drove away, mother and daughter were holding each other, but where was Henry?

After realizing that Henry was no longer standing with them, Robin shrieked in a loud voice, calling Henry and Lizzah to start crying profusely, "Daddy, oh my God, Daddy, where are you?" Henry replied with the most soothing voice, "What is y'all hollering for? I'm over here. I must have tripped on the curb or something, that's all". He stood up and hugged his wife and daughter, then unlocked the car door. After Robin was safely in the car, Henry looked at Lizzah with concern. "I'm afraid for you now," he said. "You know this was no accident, right? Somebody ain't happy about this. Is there something you want to tell me? I'm glad for your success," he said, "but I will take you home right now if your life is in danger." He told her that Hollywood and being a singer was her dream. He could not make her come home, but her safety was most important. She assured her father that she was safe and there was no need to worry.

Lizzah was angry that she, and especially her parents, had just been in a dangerous situation, and she was almost sure that Gigi had something to do with it. Lizzah began to wonder if any of them were safe.

Chapter Sixteen
A Heavy Heart

Robin sat at her kitchen table in silence. She was happy that her daughter was doing what she loved. Lizzah sounded so good, she thought to herself, and her outfit was different. All the lessons and countless hours of this child singing in her ear all day long were finally paying off. But as her mother, Robin could tell something about Lizzah wasn't quite right. She was apprehensive and not able to put her finger on it, so she began to cry.

As Henry came to sit down for dinner, he noticed Robin. Surprised by his wife's countenance, he said, "Now what's wrong with you? It would be best if you were happy for her because she's happy for a change. Her career is finally taking off good. Now you know if she wins that competition, she's going to be smelling herself, so get ready for it." "I am proud of her," Robin said, "but I'm afraid for her too". Robin looked at Henry and said, "And, Lizzah has been smelling herself for about four years now. My daughter is not at all ready for those cut-throat bigwigs in Detroit, Hollywood, or anywhere else. I mean, what is she going to be made to do to get the success she wants? Sure, she thinks she's grown and can put on makeup and sing and even dance now, but she's confused Henry! Besides, she's just a baby". Crying more now, Robin asked, "Did you see our daughter's eyes Henry? There's nothing there anymore. It's like her soul is gone". Robin crying inconsolably now said our little girl is gone.

Henry told his wife that was the craziest thing he ever heard. "That girl's soul has not gone anywhere. Her eyes are blank from smoking those funny-colored cigarettes all these kids are smoking nowadays. Robin looked at Henry, rolling her eyes in disgust. Come on, Robin, you must know she is smoking marijuana by now. That's what has been helping her perform. How else would that clumsy girl be dancing like that in front of thousands of people? I mean, she was shimmying and rocking and never did fall," Laughing really hard, Henry said. "Those cigarettes gave her some rhythm. Hell, she didn't even trip in those high-heeled shoes she was dancing in. That child was so clumsy, she done fell on every street in Chicago. Her dream is to be a successful entertainer and she is on her way. Unfortunately, I don't know if she got what it takes to be able to perform and not be high on that stuff," Henry said. "We've lost our little girl," Robin said sadly. "I don't think so," Henry said. "You know I don't care if she goes to Hollywood or not. We have not lost her, though. We've taken her to Mass all her life," Henry said. "You still go every Sunday and you pray the rosary all the time. Pray for her. Send up those Our Fathers and Hail Marys like you used to years ago for our daughter now. She is in a lifestyle where she needs them. You know, whoever was in that car the other night was sending her a message, right?" Henry said. "I do believe that Jesus will protect her. She may get a few scars, but she will be fine." As Henry left the table, he told Robin to stop worrying and get back to praying.

As Robin cleared the dinner dishes, she thought about the little bright-eyed baby she had brought home over seventeen years ago. Where had the time gone? How she loved and missed that little girl. Henry was wrong about our little girl being gone though, because the girl they had is gone. She has become a young woman overnight, it seemed. As Robin said the rosary that night, she also prayed to the Father God to bless, protect, and keep Lizzah through everything and make her soul right. As she closed her eyes, she became very calm. She knew that God had heard her and that her little Lizzah would be just fine.

Chapter Seventeen
The Final Night

When Lizzah came back inside, Sebastian and Lonnie were still up drinking Slitz Malts and Hopingaters and talking about the concert. They said they were dog-tired but could not go to sleep. When Sebastian saw Lizzah, he knew something had gone wrong. Lizzah fell into his arms instantly. She told them about the incident with her parents and the mysterious car. Simultaneously, the next word out of both of their mouths was Gigi. Lizzah told them she would let Ada Grace know first thing in the morning. Darryl overheard the conversation and came out of his room. "You know Gigi is still hanging around here. She sits in a raggedy blue car outside every day with two of dem Faces, watching everything that goes on. Darryl said that if Ada Grace didn't call the police in the morning, he would call himself. They all turned in for the night, knowing there was another big day ahead."

As each participant entered the stage, the crowd began to cheer loudly. For the announcement, most dressed in blue denim variations and white. The judges were in place looking stoic as always, and none of the entertainers had any idea which of them would be going home. The Family Malone opened the show with their popular hit single "Do What Chu Gotta Do." Johnny joined them along with Bill Brady from the Hearts of Gold.

As one of the stoic judges approached the stage, a short clip of each performance was played to remind the audience of the previous night's performances. He opens the envelope, fumbles, and drops the card on the floor. Robert Harris responds from across the room to this with a loud "Lawd Ha Mercy." We understand you don't get out much, and he laughs. Don't be nervous. It's going to be alright. The crowd laughs a little. The judge fumbles again but clumsily retrieves the envelope from the floor. He takes out his glasses, puts them on, and with a sheepish look and crackly voice says. We thought all of the performances were good. We have decided the one group that is leaving us tonight is The Georgettes with Carmelita Taylor. Stephen James took the stage and congratulated the Georgettes.

Although they would not move further in the show, they were each awarded a $5,000 stipend and transportation back to their hometown. The show continued with the Brown Sisters performing their new hit single Tears from Yesterday, followed by Gloria Gaynor's new dance song I Will

Survive. Robert Williams was next to the stage. He started by Mocking and taunting one of the judges. He went from one judge to the other, playfully staring and teasing them. Rolling his eyes, he turns away from the audience and says, "How you doin?" The stoic judge broke into a smile. He grabbed the female judge's purse and held it up. He says, "You don't mind if I look at this, do you?" She laughed and shook her head. He held it up again and looked at it. "Dis da ugliest damn purse I Eva seen in my life," and handed it back to her. He looked at the other judge and just shook his head "naw." That judge laughed. He whispered in the mike, "I just had ta see if y'all was live up hea." The crowd roared again with laughter.

The Goldwings were the first of the contestants to hit the stage. Lizzah and Johnny started their performance with Marvin Gaye's song, "Heaven must have sent you from above." When the song was about to end, Sebastian surprised the audience by throwing in a stanza of Fifth of Beethoven, and the crowd began to cheer. Abruptly, Lizzah, and Johnny broke out with Ashford and Simpson's song Solid as a Rock. Ada Grace thought it a great idea to add a short dance routine for Lizzah and Johnny before the song ended. Lizzah was not feeling the act and almost fell twice while performing. She kicked off the three-inch heels and finished her performance. The crowd was on their feet, cheering, and two of the judges were standing up, clapping this time.

The Hearts of Gold came to the stage next, singing Just My Imagination by the Temptations. They sounded good, and the crowd cheered for them. Bill was distracted for a moment when he saw Gigi in the audience with a scowl on her face. He could not help but wonder how this night would end. Trouble was in the building, he thought to himself. Not Gigi or anyone else was going to make him ruin this performance. While singing, he made his way down to the front row, kissing the hands of about eight beautiful ladies. When Bill stopped and reached for Gigi's hand, she did not oblige him but instead complained with a loud Uuuggghh. Bill smirked at her, winked, and moved on to kiss two other ladies' hands before returning to the stage.

At the end of their performance, Gigi could be heard hollering booo booo, trying to disrupt the show. Immediately, security came and escorted her and a male companion out of the building. As Robert Williams came back to the stage, he watched as Gigi was taken away. "Boy, I tell ya," he said. "Can't take some o you folk nowhere." Gigi tried to scream at him for talking about her, but security then picked her up and carried her out. As the back door slammed, Robert dropped his head and stared up at the back door, saying, "Nah don't you come back in hea now.. you hear." The crowd chuckles and on went the show.

The Soundbytes wowed the crowd by performing two songs by George Clinton and Parliament. Give up the Funk and Flashlight. They all wore metallic silver and black with sparkling pointed hats and rhinestone shoes. Near the end of their performance, they had ten dancers join them; three were suspended from mid-air. There were lights flashing and sirens going off. In a puff of smoke, their performance ended, but the band continued to play. People were dancing in the isles and having a good time. Robert Williams came back to the stage with the announcement. We gone have an out and out dance party Nah. Everybody get up out yo seat and dance. Dis roof is on fire!!

After about ten minutes of the audience dancing in the aisles and near their seats, Robert brought Stephen James to the stage. He thanked everyone for coming. He introduced each judge, and he thanked them for their financial support. The lady judge handed Stephen James an envelope. Stephen James opened the envelope, and the last group to be leaving tonight would be Darryl Genison and the Soundbytes. He congratulated them and announced that each would be getting a $10,000 stipend to assist with their career and costs. The show ended with people dancing in the aisles. The whole City of Detroit was celebrating, and people were dancing in the streets for a very long time.

Stephen James went on to announce the second-place winners would be The Goldwings with Lizzah Dee Atkins and Johnny Green and coming in First Place are Bill Brady and the Harts of Gold. Stephen James congratulates the two groups. He told them hard work now has paid off. The tour would begin in three weeks. He told them not to return home yet but to report to Jamestown Administrative Offices this coming Wednesday at 3:00 p.m. to receive further instructions. Have fun, he told everyone, and let the after-parties begin.

Lizzah could hardly believe it. She was happy and scared at the same time. Her career was taking off, and everything was happening much faster than she ever expected. She looked in the audience to see Corrine crying this time. Lizzah grabbed Corrine and brought her backstage. Carmelita and The Soundbytes joined the winners, and it was a grand celebration for them all. Lizzah used the payphone and called Robin and Henry to tell them the news. Lizzah was finally happy, but even in this, she could sense something was about to happen. She could not worry about it now because she was moving full speed ahead.

Chapter Eighteen
IT SHOULD HAVE BEEN ME

Gigi and two of The Faces, Helen and Earlene, sat in Bobby's Cocktail Lounge. Today was Gigi's birthday, and The Faces had come out to help her celebrate. They also wanted to talk with her and see what her plans were for the others. The night was just beginning, and Gigi was already drinking up everything she could get her hands on. Since being disqualified from Jamestown, Gigi has not done anything to promote them.

She was always drunk and was angry with everyone. She even blamed a few of the other Faces for her downfall. Gigi was angry with her mother, The Faces and anyone other than herself who was still breathing. Her uncle had built a gold mine for himself and, in her mind, had kicked her to the curb. At one time, Uncle Stephen used to take care of her even when her mother would not. Once her cousin, Ada Grace, showed up, all of this changed. Helen and Earlene knew this story word for word because it was all Gigi ever talked about. Since the last incident at Jamestown, Gigi's irritability had gotten much worse. It was apparent to anyone who saw her that she was angry and, well, crazy.

"There is no way that little mealy-mouthed, no-singing heifer Lizzaaaah should have won that contest! And do you know why Gigi said, slurring and hissing at the same time?" "No, why?" said the Two Faces simultaneously. "Because I am family," she said, crying profusely now. "I was cheated! I was cheated, I tell you! I am supposed to be getting ready to go to LA and Chicago and Philly, not her!" Gigi screamed. When Helen tried to tell her the truth, that it was her own fault and not anybody else, Gigi stared at her in angry disbelief.

Helen reminded Gigi that she alone got herself eliminated from the competition. She told Gigi that All Eight of them were eliminated from the contest because of her behavior. Earlene told her she lied and tried to make everyone else look bad when all she had to do was concentrate on the Faces that have always had her back. Gigi was quiet for a change as she listened to them. Neither Earlene nor Helen thought her being quiet was a good thing right now, but they had to make their voices heard, if only for the group's future. Helen told her she was not doing her job as the leader of The Faces. Gigi had made their old manager, Stewart, angry, and he flat-out refused to work with them ever again.

They reminded Gigi that she had not made any attempts to line up new work for them. Earlene told Gigi she was smoking and drinking way too much. She said the Faces' careers were almost ruined because of her behavior.

Gigi did not acknowledge any of their concerns but began ranting and raving all over again. Blood is supposed to be thicker than water! I got something for all of them, though. Just wait, and you will see. Every one of them that crossed me is going to get what they deserve! Shaking their heads, the Two Faces pleaded with Gigi one last time to pull herself together. Earlene even offered to help her detox so The Faces could recover and move past this Jamestown incident.

When Gigi did not acknowledge their concerns for the second time, the Two Faces knew what they had to do. Earlene told Gigi they would be singing with another group in Philadelphia. They would be leaving in two days and this is now goodbye. Gigi stood up quickly and then fell back down in the chair.

"Y'all are leaving me too! Okay. Okay. I got something for you too!" she screamed. As the Faces got up to leave, Gigi sat on the barstool, crying and mumbling... "It should have been me." Then she screamed into the air, "Me, I tell you!" Gigi attempted to get up to go after them and fell back down on the barstool again. As they turned to leave Bobby's Cocktail Lounge, the two former Faces looked at Gigi with both pity and disgust. "I never thought the Eight Faces of Eve would end like this," Helen said. "Happy Birthday, Gigi," Earlene mumbled, with tears in her eyes. Then, they both turned and walked out the door. They would no longer be known as one of the Faces but were looking forward to the new opportunities ahead of them.

Chapter Nineteen
LOVE SUCCESS AND TRAGEDY

Lizzah didn't plan for it to happen, but she was in love again. Life was so good lately that she often had to pinch herself to make sure this was not a dream. Although Sebastian was twelve years her senior, she doubted anyone her age would love and care for her the way he did. It made sense that they would love each other because they spent every waking moment together. Henry was not happy about this relationship at all. He said, "Sebastian was a good business partner, but he was too old." "He thought she was much too young to be getting serious with anyone, especially an old man," Henry said. Lizzah laughed at Henry and then told him that they just could not keep their hands off each other. She told him that Sebastian made it seem like she was the only woman in the world. Not wanting to hear that at all, Henry shook his head and said, "Yeah, yeah, yeah," and Lizzah laughed.

It was only six months after they won the contest, and the Goldwings had since traveled all over the US. They were popular in every State where they performed. Lizzah and Johnny did a new rendition of Only Your Love, and within one week, it was number three on the charts. The Goldwings recorded three other singles that year, and people played their songs everywhere. Life was kind to them now because The Goldwings and The Hearts of Gold were living large. Lizzah did not understand why Sebastian was not happy with Jamestown and Pappa J because they were making a lot of money. He always complained to Ada Grace about their contract. When Sebastian told Ada Grace about the contract offer from Finnabe Records, Stephen reluctantly agreed to increase their cut to seventy-five percent. This made Sebastian happy for a little while. Sebastian complained about everything, she thought.

Going forward, it was Sebastian who kept Lizzah safe from the politics and nonsense of the industry. She was his Queen, and everybody knew it; even Papa J. Sebastian had found out about Papa J's reputation for seducing young girls. It was rumored that any female who achieved success in Jamestown had to have gotten to know Pappa J at one time or another. The problem was he loved Lizzah and vowed that this old man would never lay a hand on her. He was grateful that Ada Grace and Lizzah were best friends, and he thought this may be why he had not come after her before now. His eyes were beginning to roam whenever

Lizzah was around, and Sebastian knew it would only be a matter of time before he pulled something. The other problem was that Lizzah didn't have the slightest clue about this potential problem, and when he tried to tell her, she did not believe him.

Because he was the eldest member of the Goldwings, Sebastian took on the role of Group Manager. He worked closely with Ada Grace and the rest of the Jamestown staff, making sure their sound was right. At rehearsals, he made sure everyone was doing their best work. Although Sebastian was always intoxicated, he monitored everyone's drug use and alcohol intake. Because of Sebastian, all of them functioned very well on cloud nine. Ralph was the only sober one in the group. He did not smoke or drink alcoholic beverages, but he always had a Pepsi Cola bottle, a Suzy Q, and a bag of Jay's Potato Chips in his hand. When anyone teased him about it, he would laugh and say, hey, you got your vice. I've got mine.

Before each show, Ralph prayed, and after the show was over, he read his Bible. Ralph prayed with everyone about everything. Pretty soon, people realized that God heard when Ralph prayed, and everything was going to work out. Ralph was known to everyone at Jamestown as Preacher Boy, and even Pappa J respected him. Everyone was happy and doing well. For the rest of the year, they performed, traveled, and they got high. Life is so sweet, Lizzah thought to herself. She did not even entertain the idea that Sebastian may be right about his suspicions about Pappa J. She was looking forward to spending the holidays with her family and friends.

Everyone was excited to spend Christmas with their families, and Ralph had started to reconcile with his family. He decided to spend the holidays at home and with his church family. Lonnie and Ronnie went to see their parents at their new home in South Bend. Lizzah, Ada Grace, and Corrine spent a few days on Chicago's Mag Mile, then spent the holiday with Robin and Henry. Sebastian stayed in Calumet City with his parents, but he would somehow end up at Robin and Henry's house every day. Robin was so excited to host all the little superstars, and Henry was just beside himself with joy. On Christmas Eve, Sebastian and Henry spun records all day, and Sebastian even had Henry singing Christmas Carrols. That's when they found out that Henry could actually sing. The younger ladies wrapped presents and trimmed the tree while

Robin and Lizzah's Aunts cooked and finished touches on the lights outside.

On Christmas Day, the family came in from Michigan, Canada, and Ohio. Everyone was dancing and singing, having a good time. More family came over along with Lizzah's Auntie Betty and Uncle Alvin.

Everyone loved them because they would play fight and argue with each other all day long. Everyone around them could tell that they loved each other very much, but they were the life of the party everywhere they went. Lonnie, Ronnie, and Darryl stopped by, and everyone ate and drank and were so full of food. It was hard for any of them to move. I had the best Christmas ever, Lizzah told her Mom. Thank you for letting my friends come over. Robin hugged her daughter and said, "Anytime."

The next day was a Sunday, so everyone went to early Mass. They returned to Robin and Henry's house for breakfast. Lizzah was so excited to have her friends over that she forgot to warn everyone about their Sunday breakfast tradition. Of course, Robin would tell everyone about those brains and eggs and the story behind them. Lizzah was embarrassed at first, but to her surprise, everyone loved them. Sunday breakfast at Robin and Henry's house would be an event everyone talked about for years to come.

On Monday, Lizzah, Corrine, and Ada Grace decided to spend the last day of their Christmas vacation together at the Pick Congress Hotel. They decided to have brunch in the Walnut Room. This was one of Corrine's favorite places to go during the holidays. They all went to a movie before dropping Corrine at the airport for her early evening flight. Lizzah and Ada Grace went back to the hotel to pack and get some sleep. When they arrived at their room, there was an urgent message from Ralph for Lizzah to call his parent's house. While Lizzah showered, Ada Grace returned the call and immediately began screaming. Lizzah, finding her best friend crying, took the phone from her and spoke to Ralph herself. She learned that their beloved Johnny had been killed in a car accident on Christmas night. His Brougham was one of two cars that were mangled by a jackknifed semi, and neither Johnny nor his girlfriend had survived. Instead of going to bed for some much-needed rest, everyone met at

Johnny's Mother's house to console his family. How could she console them, Lizzah thought, when she needed so much consolation herself. She and Johnny had been making beautiful music together since the beginning of their careers. Every time she thought of them never again performing together, she began to cry.

Neither Lizzah nor Ada Grace said anything on the way to the airport. This hurts so bad, Lizzah thought to herself. How will her heart ever recover from this? She had so many questions and not one answer. How could they ever replace Johnny, and how long would it take even to try to duplicate his sound? One thing was certain. The Goldwings would go on, and she had to go on as well.

Chapter Twenty
Cost of Success

The more they traveled, the greater was the demand for public appearances. Television shows were eager to have them in their studios so they could satisfy the public outcry. The Goldwings appeared on Grandstand America one week, while the Hearts of Gold traveled to Portland to appear on The Party Plain. They had engagements scheduled every weekend until June. Lizzah was grieving, and she was exhausted.

Pappa J had chosen a neighborhood talent (Solomon) to replace Johnny. Solomon had a good voice. He sounded almost like Johnny and learned the material quickly, but for the Goldwings, he was bad news. Solomon sang with them three times and was already fighting with Sebastian. He was never on time for rehearsals, and when he got there, all he did was complain.

Solomon complained about the suits they wore. He said they made him look like a clown. Sebastian told him none of them were happy about how Jamestown made them dress, but they were now a part of the brand. That brand is a big part of everyone's success. Solomon complained about everything from the water in the dressing room not being cold enough, and he wanted to only be at rehearsals on certain days. Most of the time, everyone ignored his rantings. Neither the Goldwings nor the Hearts of Gold got along with him. The only way Solomon blended with the group was in song.

Solomon had a drinking problem, and it was quickly spiraling out of control. He would only sing with the Goldwings for six months before getting arrested for beating up his former girlfriend. Pappa J jumped on that opportunity and immediately replaced him. Because there was an urgent need to find a replacement, Papa J did something he swore he would never ever do. He gave a golden opportunity to a voice he had never heard.

Mark Brown loved Jamestown. Ever since he was a young teenager, he and his friends would hang around in front of Jamestown each day after school. Mark thought that if he came around often, Mr. James would see how serious he was about an audition. Over the years, Mark had given the staff over one hundred audio tapes of his group and some solo recordings. Each time, they dismissed him as an annoying kid and put his tapes in the trash. They often joked about how annoying he was and how long it would take for him to give up and go away. Nobody, not even Ada Grace, ever even considered bringing him inside to hear him. Once in community college, Mark would only come around about once a week. When they saw him in front of the building on this day talking with friends, Ada Grace suggested they could at least give him a try. Out of sheer desperation, Pappa J handed him a tape. He demanded he come back and be prepared to sing the male lead vocals of all the songs. To everyone's surprise, he sounded good. It helped that he was a good dancer. He also had a good stage presence, and the girls all said he was extremely nice-looking.

Mark did not sound at all like Johnny or Solomon. His voice was a little rougher and more raspy than Johnny. To everyone's surprise, the blend worked well. They tweaked the sound a little bit, and Mark and Lizzah sounded well together. Mark was glad to be part of the group. He was easy to get along with, and everyone was once again a family.

The Goldwings continued to tour and were popular everywhere they went. They released four new singles that year, with one song, "Step Back on My Love," making it to the top two this time. Mark somehow managed to tour and take a class each semester. He was the second member of the Goldwings who did not smoke or drink. He and Ralph spent a lot of time together.

It was finally happening. Lizzah had finished the required coursework and was graduating from high school with her class. She had a few weeks off from touring, so graduation came at the right time. Robin tried to convince her to take college classes while she continued to travel, but Lizzah did not have it in her. She was tired of school, and her career was in full swing, or so she thought. Lizzah decided to skip prom because bringing Sebastian would draw a lot of extra attention. She just wanted to pick up her diploma and leave without fanfare, but the dean convinced her to participate in the ceremony. She decided to go to the lunchroom while waiting for graduation rehearsals to begin.

She spotted her classmate Trisha in the corner with her head down, crying and writing profusely. Lizzah was confused because Trisha was the sanctified girl who was always happy but always got into trouble. Either she was hiding a relationship with a boyfriend her mom didn't like or getting suspended for slapping a teacher. Trisha was a bit peculiar, and It was puzzling to Lizzah how she had lasted long enough to graduate. Lizzah sat with her and waited for this sob story to begin. Trisha said she was in trouble because she was missing a writing assignment in literature class. Her teacher, Mr. Haggman, would not let her graduate if she didn't turn it in within the hour. Trisha had another class to go to and did not have time to do the work. Lizzah told her to go to class and that she would write the paper for her. When Trisha gave it to her teacher later that day, she got an excellent grade. Trisha was so thankful that she invited Lizzah to her mother's church and said they could probably go out for dinner afterward. Lizzah reluctantly agreed to visit her church before going back on tour.

The day before graduation, Ada Grace and Corrine met Lizzah in Chicago. They went shopping for outfits to wear to the jazz club and a few other places. Lizzah had decided to wear her mother's clothes out of the house and do an outfit switcharoo at the club, just like old times. After shopping, they stopped by the Sheraton to eat lunch at the Kontiki Port. Once again, they had a ball on the Mag Mile, which was becoming one of Ada Grace's places to hang out. They all spent the night at Lizzah's house so they could go with her to the ceremony. The graduation ceremony went by quickly as there were only 200 graduates. Corrine was happy to see some of her old classmates and vowed to get together with them before leaving town.

Ada Grace was a little sad because it reminded her of some of the opportunities she hadn't taken advantage of in her own life. Lizzah was amazed at the number of classmates that were graduating that she didn't know. It was only God's grace and her mother's prayers she was walking across this stage, she thought to herself.

The following Sunday, they went to early Mass and came to Robin and Henry's traditional breakfast. Since it was still early, Lizzah decided to go and visit Trisha's Mother's church. She promised her classmate she would stop by, and she wanted to keep her word. Corrine and Ada Grace thought it was a good idea. Before going to Mass with Lizzah, they had not been to church in years.

Nothing could have prepared these ladies for what they were about to see. The church was in the basement of Trisha's Mother's home, and it was tiny. There were no church attendees this Sunday but the three of them, and it did not take long for them to see why. The stairs were painted with red, yellow, and green stripes, and strange statutes lined the porch. Candles and incense were burning all over the place. Four metal chairs lined a small space in the basement, and Rev. Worley stood behind a small podium that looked of cheap gold. Trisha introduced them to her mother, and she welcomed them at first. After Rev. Worley found out about Lizzah and Ada Grace being in the entertainment business, the atmosphere changed.

After that, all she talked about was the fire and brimstone. According to her, all of them were going to hell. She spoke about the way they dressed and their lifestyle. She told Lizzah that her God didn't bless people who sang secular music. Said she should give up her career and come and join her church. She taunted Ada Grace for having a rich father who was a sinner, saying she would have to pay for her sins and that only Jesus could save her.

Finally, Ada Grace got up abruptly and stumbled to the door. "I have the worst headache," she said to Rev. Worley, rolling her eyes at Trisha. "We have to go now," she said to her friends. Within seconds, Lizzah and Corrine were up and were right behind her. Trisha ran after them, profusely apologizing for the rant her mother had just made. They all could not wait to get out of there, and Corrine said it was the spookiest thing she had ever seen. Lizzah was confused as well, wondering why doing what she loved most would make her go to hell. Each of them was confused, and all agreed they felt terrible, especially coming from church. When they got to Robin's house, she prayed for them and blessed each of them with olive oil. Ada Grace was holding her head, trying to make the pain stop. Robin gave her an aspirin and a cup of warm milk. They talked for hours about God and the Bible, and Robin told them to stay away from that crazy Dragon Lady preacher and her weird daughter. They laughed about it but would later think about the lesson they learned that day for a very long time.

The Goldwings were on to Philadelphia, and Sebastian was edgier than ever. He was never mean to Lizzah, but lately, he was overprotective, and she could not understand why. They spent every moment together. Every time Lizzah went anywhere without him, it was the same drill. Stay alert and away from the promoters and camera people for a while. Now, he was mad at her for smoking too much. He talked about Pappa J all the time now. He said he did not like the way he looked at her. Lizzah thought to herself that Sebastian needed to lighten up.

When she mentioned it to Ada Grace, she confirmed that Sebastian was correct, and yes, she should listen to him and, indeed, watch her back. She told Lizzah that her father had slept with every female he had promoted and that he was ruthless. He wanted to come for you six months ago but promised me that he would leave you alone. At this news, Lizzah was surprised and very disappointed. The very thought of sleeping with Papa J was disgusting to her.

I am the oldest of at least sixteen siblings with about ten different women, Ada Grace explained. He and my mother were childhood sweethearts. My Mom helped him build his business, and when he found out she was pregnant with me, he dumped her like a hot potato. Said he could be tied down raising no kid. After they split up, he did not talk to her or help her. My mother was nineteen years old and had to get on welfare. We were broke for a very long time. I was twelve years old when I found out who my father was. I mean, I could not believe it. I wanted to know why my mother and I lived in poverty and my father was a millionaire. Against my mother's wishes, I came to Jamestown to see my father. He refused to even see me at first. After I came back the second time, he invited me in. I think my Aunt Lottie had something to do with that because she has been nice to me from day one. When he found out I could sing and had an ear for music, he put me to work.

Although I've never held a job outside of Jamestown, I've been able to buy my mother a house and she has gone back to college. My father has never given my mother a dime except through me. I am the only one of the sixteen siblings he openly acknowledges. It's a good thing that you are all getting positive exposure now because, mark my words, this thing will get ugly for both groups. The only reason he has not come after you is because we're friends. He promised me he would leave you alone for now. We have to get you signed up with another agency right when the contract ends. The Hearts might have a chance since there are no women in that group. Your "Papa J" only lets you go so far, and then all the ladies have to pay the piper or be cut off.

Lizzah was speechless. "I'll have to let Sebastian know he was right, I guess." She was still in shock at what she had just learned. "Sebastian knows everything," Ada Grace replied. "You now know, well, just about everything. There is one other sibling that I didn't mention. You cannot tell anyone, but it's Gigi." "Wait! What!" Lizzah said. "Your cousin Gigi that was in the show?" Yep said Ada Grace. "I thought Gigi's mother was Pappa J's sister," Lizzah said. She replied to Ada Grace, "Soooo Pappa J had a child by his sister?" Ada Grace looked at Lizzah, nodded, and said, "Now you know."

CHAPTER TWENTY-ONE
BAD SECRETS

Ralph could not eat or sleep. He usually did not worry about anything because God had blessed him beyond what he could ever imagine. Now, no matter how he prayed, he could not shake this horrible feeling of fear. Something was about to happen, and it was not going to be good. He was having dreams of snakes with human faces on them. In his last dream, they were performing, and everyone in the audience had a snake's body, but the faces were familiar to him. He knew deep down this could not be good. He prayed for God to protect all of them, but he still struggled with that horrible feeling of fear and dread. Not my will, Lord, but your will be done, was his daily prayer.

On the July Fourth weekend, Pappa J was to host his Annual Holiday Gala. Neither Sebastian nor Lizzah were surprised to learn that she was the only one of his entertainers invited to the Gala. Pappa J had requested that the invitation remain a secret and that nobody, not even his daughter could know about it. He told Lizzah he wanted to introduce her to some important people. These people could take her career beyond what she could ever imagine. She did not dare tell Robin and Henry because they would make her come home. Pappa J even sent her a dress and shoes to wear that night. The dress was so skimpy it was like wearing nothing at all. She was excited and nervous at the same time.

Lizzah knew deep down what Pappa J wanted from her, and the very thought of it made her sick to her stomach. If she refused his invitation, it could be an abrupt end to not only her career but also the Goldwings. Ada Grace would know what to do. She was sure of it. She could not understand why there was no answer at her house, and she had not seen her for a few days.

Sebastian was furious with Pappa J, and the very thought of him or any other man putting their hands on Lizzah was making him insane. He was so in love with her, and this situation was getting ugly quickly. How can he protect the love of his life from this powerful, wealthy music giant and still have a recording contract? He had worked so hard for his career, and he intended to slay this giant. They had to develop a plan, and they had to do it quickly. They had to find Ada Grace. The Gala was in two days, and their plan had to not only work but also be sensible.

Lizzah and Sebastian decided to go by Ada Grace's house. When they arrived, they found her disheveled. She had been beaten and she was deeply depressed. She said she had just been sitting there and had not called anyone or answered the phone. Her place was torn up and all her glass furniture was in pieces. It turns out that her ex-boyfriend, Cedric had thwarted Jamestown security and walked directly inside her house. He begged her to take him back, vowing he still loved her. Said he no longer had a place to stay and needed to stay there until he could sober up. When Ada Grace flat-out refused and asked him to leave, he took advantage of her and hit her. She had not gone to the police or reported the incident because Cedric promised to kill her if he was ever questioned or arrested about what happened. Ada Grace said she just took a lot of showers, waited, and then took more showers.

Sebastian, not knowing what else to do, left Lizzah with Ada Grace to help console her. They cleaned up the place and got everything back together. No matter how she pleaded with her, Lizzah could not convince Ada Grace to go to the police.

Sebastian called an emergency meeting with the Goldwings to fill them in on Pappa J's request. They were all upset and Mark, the newest member of the Goldwings, was in shock. None of them knew what to do, but they all agreed they could not just do nothing. They said the Jamestown property was large enough that all of them could be on the house grounds and not be detected. All of them would be on the property that night except Preacher Boy. His job would be to pray. They decided that Lizzah would go to the party. When things started to get heated, she would fake sick and call Sebastian to come and get her. None of them could imagine nor prepare for what was to be one of the most dreadful nights of their lives.

Even in the turmoil she was going through with Cedric, Ada Grace could sense something was not quite right with Lizzah. What is happening, she asked her friend. When Lizzah explained everything, Ada Grace was furious. She said her father had requested she go to Pittsburgh for a holiday gathering. So he would get her off the scene and out of town so he could do his dirt. The bastard has decided to have his way with you after all. When Sebastian came to pick Lizzah up, he told them about their plan for that night.

"That won't work!" Ada Grace told them. "It is not enough for everyone to be on the grounds and have Lizzah inside with my father! You still don't have a clue who we're dealing with, do you? If my father wants you, he will not stop until he gets what he wants. If he even feels you are resisting, he will drug you and take it, and for money, he will let others have a piece of you too. He is a ruthless bastard who does not stop until he gets what he wants. Get this through your head! Pappa J does not care about anyone but himself and making money. You are not special to him, and you are replaceable. After you all make him all the money, he will toss you aside like a dirty rag doll and go to his next adventure. There have been some girls who played the game right, and he took excellent care of them. You, Lizzah, are not that type."

"I love you, Ada Grace, but I must ask why you are helping me and are not being loyal to your father. Don't you love him?" Ada Grace was hurt by the question at first but decided it was fair. "Lizzah, you are my little sister. Even if we don't share the same blood, you will always be my sister because you are genuine. To answer your question, no, I do not love my father. I wanted a relationship with him at first, but now I just want his money. Nobody knows Mr. Stephen James the way my Aunt Lottie and I do. Why was my mother on Welfare and he was a millionaire? To this day, he has not given my mother a dime to take care of us. I hate that bastard," said Ada Grace, "And I plan to take him for everything I can, then get out of the game. I cannot believe I'm saying this but go to the party. Don't eat or drink anything while you're there."

"He will probably have you mingle and meet his friends before he tries anything. You are to come in not feeling well. I mean, you got a headache, stomachache, and the real flu bug. After fifteen minutes, you tell him you must leave and that you don't feel well and can hardly stand up. You have to be really sick. Fake it to the point that you throw up on everyone if you must. Stagger out the door and get off the premises quickly." She told Sebastian he needed to be as close to the door as he could get. "I will be in town that night despite Dad's little scheme." Ada Grace sarcastically suggested that Lizzah get her hair, nails, and makeup done and get ready for her date. Ada Grace left the house at the same time as Lizzah and

Sebastian. She told them she would call them later that night. She said she had a police report to file.

Neither Lizzah nor Sebastian heard from Ada Grace on the day of the Gala. She still trusted her friend to come through for her because Ada Grace always did. Although there were a few hundred people at the party, Sebastian, Mark, Ronnie, and Lonnie drove through the back of the grounds undetected. They were surprised to see Darryl there and had no idea how he found out about the plan. Darryl said he heard Lizzah was in trouble and that we could use a little help. On the other side of the house, there was a group of people setting up a massive fireworks display.

Lizzah was nervous, anxious, and had the worst headache. Sebastian escorted her to the door and reluctantly helped her take off her coat, revealing the skimpy dress. She was so self-conscious and Sebastian gave her a lengthy kiss before she walked through the doors. Sebastian tried to come in with her but was denied because he didn't have an invitation. The first thing Lizzah noticed when she got inside was the plethora of drugs and alcohol available just for the taking. People were dancing in the main ballroom. Some strange noises were coming from a room off to the side of the entryway. A strobe light and a black light were going, and Lizzah's head was pounding. There was no food to be had but trays of pills, white packets, and slim cigarettes of rainbow colors. After she stood in the entryway for a few minutes, a man in a suit jacket came and escorted her upstairs. He told her that Mr. James and a few of his guests were waiting for her.

The thought of what she may be walking into nearly made her knees buckle. She gained her footing, held her head high, and walked boldly into the room. Seated were Pappa J and two music professionals, Mr. Warren Williams, a professor from Hobart, Indiana, and Hiram Blandon, the CEO of The Los Angeles Music Conservatory. Lizzah was feeling sick now because Papa J and one of his friends looked at her like she was fresh meat. The older man nodded to her when Pappa J introduced them. He looked at her with disgust, probably because she had on very few clothes. She thought she also saw a look of compassion on his face.

Outside on the Lawn

Sebastian joined Lonnie, Ronnie, Mark, and Darryl on the north lawn. They were quietly waiting for Lizzah to come out when Anthony "Butter" Jackson, Stephen James' head officer, confronted them. Butter told them they could not be there. He said, "Unless y'all can show me an invitation that you have cause to be here, you got to leave now." Sebastian explained to him that Lizzah was his fiancé and had a meeting with Mr. James. She is not feeling well. He said his fiancée accepted Mr. James' invitation but is going to cut the session short and come home. He was staying to take her home. Butter chuckled and, with a wide grin showing all his thirty-two gold teeth, said, "I hate to break it to you, but if your woman is with Mr. James, she's not coming out of there no time soon. She'll get back atcha sometime tomorrow." "Laughing louder now," he said, "she ain't coming out tonight!" Lonnie, Mark and Sebastian went back and forth with them for a bit. Butter turned serious in a split second, then put his hand on a gun. He told Sebastian, "Face it, man, your woman ain't coming out, and you aint going in." "Mocking Sebastian and laughing," he said, "Aww man, she'll be back." Butter started laughing once again. Just when Sebastian went to grab Butter by his throat, Lonnie grabbed Sebastian to hold him back. Instantly, the grounds lit up with thunderous fireworks. At the same time, a house closer to the South Lawn exploded and went up in flames. There was no place they could run because chaos was all around them. They could still see Butter laughing and waving his gun around. Then everything went black. There were no more fireworks, no menacing Butter. Nothing.

CHAPTER TWENTY-ONE

In The House

After talking for about fifteen minutes, Papa J and his friends excused themselves briefly and went to another room of the house. Lizzah tried to make her way downstairs to the door without being noticed. That plan didn't work, and she was escorted back upstairs by one of the house assistants. This time, she was taken to Papa J's private parlor. Lizzah wanted to run away, but she could not move. Her head was spinning now, and she was having trouble keeping her balance. Pappa J greeted Lizzah in a silk bathrobe. She was pretty sure he didn't have anything on under that robe. He grabbed her hand and pulled it to his bare chest. Then he kissed her hand. I've been waiting a long time for us to spend some quality time together. Lizzah told him she really didn't want him to get the wrong idea. She told him that she and Sebastian were planning to be married soon. Still grabbing her hand and moving too close for Lizzah's comfort, Pappa J congratulated her on the engagement. He told her she was family and he offered to pay for her wedding. "I take care of my family," Pappa J said, "Especially family that takes care of me."

Lizzah attempted to back up, telling Pappa J that she really didn't feel well and how badly her head was hurting right now. Pappa J discretely grabbed two pills, a blue one and a red one. He put both pills on the tip of his tongue and closed his mouth. He grabbed Lizzah and began to stroke her thighs. As much as she wanted to, she could not move. Her head hurt, and all she wanted to do was go to sleep. Pappa J grabbed Lizzah and started stroking her breast. His hand moved quickly from her buttocks and back to her breasts. Again, she attempted to resist him by pushing away from him, but to no avail.

The stench of Old Spice, cigars, and hair pomade was making her even more sick every minute. When Lizzah tried again to push away from him, Pappa J picked her up and sat her on top of his desk. As he forced her legs open, he kissed her, transferring the two pills from his mouth to hers. Pappa J whispered this will alleviate that headache, trust me. You won't feel any pain in a minute. In a flash, her dress was off, and Pappa J had entered her. Lizzah drifted in and out of consciousness. Each time she woke up, she could hear Papa J and his friends talking. They were teasing the older gentleman because he had refused to partake with them.

As she drifted out of consciousness again, she heard the older man scolding Papa J. This girl is only a child-man. "Shame on you," he said. "Why, she's young enough to be .. my daughter. I'll pass," he said. Lizzah thought of Sebastian and how angry he would be with her. Clearly, she had failed to hold up her end of the deal, she thought to herself. She wondered why Ada Grace had not come to see about her and if she was okay. Where were Sebastian and the others? Did Ada Grace go out of town after all? Still, she trusted her friend. While Pappa J had his way with her repeatedly, she could not move. She could not fight, nor could she run. The only thing Lizzah was able to do was to think and sleep.

Chapter Twenty-Two
MAD HOLIDAY

Robin had not heard from Lizzah in over a week. She was concerned because, until now, her daughter had made her way to Chicago on every holiday. They talked to each other every week. As she put away the leftover food, Henry called her from the basement, "Look at the news," he said. "Robin! Come now!" Startled by the command, she ran to see what was going on. It must be something serious, she thought, because Henry never gets this upset. Channel Seven news showed the Jamestown Mansion and Pappa J along with thirty others that were arrested. The news anchor said Pappa J was distributing various illegal drugs during his Annual Holiday Gala.

After police entered the home, they found one female naked and unconscious. Her name and current condition are not known. Robin's heart sank, but she kept listening. While the people were inside the house, chaos was happening all around them on the outside.

Apparently, at the same time, four people have been shot by Jamestown grounds security, and it has been confirmed that one has died. The four who were shot were trying to enter the Gala without an invitation. It appears they were all shot by grounds security. We don't have any information on the names of the victims or their condition. At the exact time the gunfire was being exchanged, a cottage home located on the grounds exploded. That home belongs to Ada Grace James, who is the daughter of the music industry giant. While the daughter was not home at the time of the explosion, she is hospitalized in serious condition from an earlier domestic incident. Cedric Jones, a former boyfriend, and a cousin, Gianja Terry, are currently being questioned in connection to that crime. The guests inside the house were not aware of anything until the police entered Stephen James's home. We will give you more information once we receive it.

"Where is Lizzah???" Robin said, screaming. "She is not answering her phone!!!" Robin and Henry sat there in shock. Henry hung his head, saying, "I should have made that girl come home last year when somebody almost ran me over." Robin snapped back at Henry, saying, "I don't how you think you could have convinced her to come home. You couldn't even convince her to stay in school. I'm getting too old for this!"

Robin snapped, "Now I don't know if she will ever be coming home!" Robin cried, "She will be home, trust me," Henry said. They said nothing as they simultaneously started throwing stuff in suitcases. Within a half-hour, they were on the road to Michigan. The first stop is Jamestown.

Chapter Twenty-Three
Prison Woes

(The Agony of Lizzah's First Love)

TJ lay in his bunk, sad and distraught. He had played their song over forty-five times that day, and his cellmates were not happy with him at all. They dared not say anything to him about the music because he clearly was not in a good mood. He had tried to find out what was going on, but nobody on the outside had any information for him.

After the Jamestown incident, it seemed Lizzah and the Goldwings had all just disappeared.

Every day, he thought of her and the beautiful time they shared together. He wanted to see her so badly each time she tried to visit. He refused to see her because he knew it would just open a big can of worms. He wanted her to go on and live her life because she deserved that. Lizzah was so young and innocent. He was glad to hear that she kept her promise and finished school. TJ listened to the radio whenever he could and even bought all the songs she and the Goldwings made. She recorded their song "Only Your Love," and it reached number three on the charts. Lizzah must have started putting money on his books a while back because it just kept coming. Nobody can tell him exactly where the money was coming from. One thing was sure: it had made his life in Straightertville much easier. That girl is so special, and she was once mine. If only I had made better choices, he thought.

As painful as it was to know she had found someone else, TJ always thought she would be safe. What was this Sebastian guy doing that he didn't protect his Queen from that sick bastard, he thought. James would soon be family from the looks of things, and he would get his just due. TJ only hoped that he could do it personally now. He was hurt, and he was angry. Nobody had any news about who had been injured or who had been killed. For Lizzah's sake, he had hoped it was not Sebastian. He had to believe his Queen would make it through this. Remembering what the Chaplain talked about this past Sunday, he asked God to help Lizzah and everyone involved. In TJ's mind, he was her husband, even though they were far apart. He trusted that God heard his prayer and that Lizzah would be safe. The only real comfort he had now was to listen to their song. He still believed he would hold her again one day.

Only Your Love
Only your Love can Wooo me.. It soothes me .. improves me
Your kiss It makes me. It breaks me and overtakes me
How am I supposed to live without you
What I gotta do to get through to you
Ohh Ohh Ohh I wish that I could hold you now
Gotta find a way how
I really want to see your face
Feel your sweet embrace
Oohh Ohh Ohh I really need to talk to you
Tell me just what to do
So you and me can ever be
One through eternity....

CHAPTER TWENTY-FOUR
MELISSA'S PLEA

(Intervention from an Ancestor—See Intro One)

Melissa was in deep trouble. She had stepped out of the Order and quickly spiraled downward toward Earth's atmosphere. Her biggest mistake was leaving Nirvana, even only for a millisecond. Now, she could not find her way back, no matter how she tried. She was deeply grieved because she simply could not forget what she had just witnessed.

The young maiden was surrounded by so many vile and contentious beings. Abbadon was undoubtedly at work here, and things have gotten so wicked that it grieved her soul. She hated Abbadon because all he had ever done was destroy the good. For centuries, he has confused God's people. Many of them never experience the good things the father has for them because of his deception.

Melissa only wanted to see the young maiden find her way to righteousness and earn her passage to Nirvana. After all, isn't this why God created each one of us, to worship and come into the oneness of him? Now, for the first time in centuries, she was lost and could not find her way back. As she continued to descend, fear and doubt took hold of her. Melissa had not experienced these two vile creatures in years. She feared she would never meet her earthly offspring and now doubted she could ever get back to Nirvana.

She sensed the presence of Gabriel all around her. Although his Presence was always soothing to her, Melissa was not ready to face Gabriel just yet, as she had descended on so many levels. Suddenly, Gabriel grabbed her in his arms, breaking her fall. She thought he would be angry with her, but he was very kind. "Why are you troubled, my dear?" he asked. "Did you step out of the protective realm where the father has placed you?" As she tried to answer, Gabriel put his finger to her lips. "You asked God to grant him a second chance, and he did. Do you not trust God to fulfill the promise he made to you? What were you hoping to see by stepping out of your place of assignment?" Again, he put his finger to her lips, not even expecting an answer.

"Do not be troubled any longer, for the father has sent me to you with words of truth and comfort. The young maiden is sleeping now," Gabriel said. She has been harmed in her physical body, yes, but her soul still lives.

This will be a life-changing lesson for her. This is not her time to depart the earth. She will learn from this, and you will see that her life will never be the same. God's blessings on her life are just beginning to flourish, but she can only receive them if she makes the right choices.

Now you, dear Melissa, must return at once into the joy of our Lord. Do not leave Nirvana ever again because there is no guarantee you will be able to return next time. At Gabriel's release, she ascended rapidly, returning to her eternal place of rest.

Chapter Twenty-Five
Peace and Victory

Several months following the incident at Jamestown, Ralph fell into a deep state of depression. His life was suddenly crumbling in pieces, he thought. There were no more Goldwings. They lost poor Ronnie that night and almost lost Lonnie and Sebastian. He cried each time he thought of Lizzah and what she must have endured inside that mansion. He should have been there, too, that night. But no, they insisted he stay home and pray. Oh, how he prayed for all of them. How could God let this happen, he thought, and now, suddenly, God goes silent. He questioned his faith. Did he ever hear from God in the first place? In his mind, he had let the Goldwings down, and it hurt so bad.

Two years after the incident, Ralph's parents became terminally ill. They called him to come home to pastor The Open-Door ministry. Reluctantly, he obliged. He asked Sebastian to run the music department and Lizzah to direct the choir and sing. Lizzah was skeptical at first because she did not have much experience singing church music. She had to admit that mysterious, wonderful things happened when she and Sebastian performed the songs and that she was very happy now. When they first came to The Open-Door ministry, Sebastian would play, and Lizzah would sing and teach harmony to the eight choir members. Within a year, the church had grown to about two hundred members, and now, there were eighty voices in the choir.

There was standing room only as people filled the auditorium for the pre-Christmas program. Lizzah did not know if people were coming because they were once famous and wanted to be a part of them, or if these people really loved the Lord and wanted to change their lives.

She knew she no longer cried when she thought about that dreadful night at Jamestown. That awful night, they lost poor Ronnie and almost lost Sebastian and Lonnie.

As she looked at the choir marching in, she could not help but be thankful to God for how he had completely turned her life around. She and Sebastian had been so busy with their new twin daughters, Lauren and Allyssa, that just about everything else had taken a back seat.

Sebastian dotted on his daughters. Everyone marveled at how much the two girls favored their Aunt Ada Grace. Sebastian and Lizzah dismissed the skeptics and were proud and loving parents.

The choir was becoming popular, and churches all over were asking them to sing in their programs. Lizzah and Sebastian were so busy preparing the music and parenting they had no time to dwell on any of their past hurts and negativity.

Even from prison, Stephen James was still trying to negotiate a new record contract, sending his cronies to the church. They said James needed their help, and he wanted a fresh start. Not one of them paid him any attention. Little did Stephen James know that Lizzah, Sebastian, and all the others had already received their fresh start. God had fixed their hearts, and Jamestown Corporation had settled each of their pockets with a sixty-million-dollar settlement. Ada Grace helped them all win.

Three Years Later

Despite everything she has endured, Lizzah still loves to sing and is now giving God the praise. Lizzah, Corrine and Ada Grace are still good friends and business partners. Lizzah is glad that Ada Grace has turned her life over to Christ and is safe from that stalker ex-boyfriend of hers. Ada Grace invested a portion of her settlement in launching a Gospel label called Praise N Glory's Presence to promote gospel choirs and solo artists. Lizzah and Sebastian would go on to release the first album on the Label. The song "Praising in His Secret Place" would come to be one of the most popular praise songs worldwide.

Finally, Lizzah can say that she loves her life, and she loves to sing about it. She vowed to cherish this life to her last breath and to be a light source of encouragement to everyone she meets.

The End.

About the Author

Jannise R. Childs was born in Los Angeles, California. When she was two, her parents moved to Chicago, Illinois, where she currently resides. Growing up, she was fascinated with music. She loved to sing, model and dance. As she grew older, she also developed a love for writing poetry and novels. As a teenager and young adult, she performed with many small groups. Throughout the years, she has been a soprano voice in many church choirs. Jannise has been gainfully employed as an administrative professional for most of her adult life.

In her first book, A Songbird Story, a Singer's Intense Battle for her Soul, Jannise shows how factual past events, a young girl's hopes and dreams, mixed with a lot of imagination, can tell a wonderful story. As before, Jannise is confident you will enjoy this new version, A Young Songbird's Story, even more. She is confident you will enjoy this experience with the turn of each page.

Jannise R. Childs

A Young Songbird's Story:
A Singers Battle for Her Soul

Jannise R. Childs

www.ingramcontent.com/pod-product-compliance
Lightning Source LLC
Chambersburg PA
CBHW071156130726
47998CB00002B/522